A WILL OF HER OWN

A WILL OF
HER OWN

•

Patricia DeGroot

AVALON BOOKS
NEW YORK

PRINTED IN THE UNITED STATES OF AMERICA
ON ACID-FREE PAPER
BY HADDON CRAFTSMEN, BLOOMSBURG, PENNSYLVANIA

SEP 18 2002 RH

To my mother,
Norma Rae Hutchings Bowman Mahoney.
For starting the journey.

Prologue

Deep Winter, Colorado, 1860

The fire did nothing to warm the cabin.

The wind blew too hard, pressing frigid air through the cracks and crevices of the wood-slate walls, and swirling fast-falling snow up against the worn exterior in high drifts.

Still, April Wilde tossed another log on the hearth, determined to stop her mother's shivering.

"April? We're waiting for you."

April turned at the sound of her mother's raspy voice, barely audible above the angry tempest outside. The sight sent another chill coursing through her twelve-year-old frame. Sarah Wilde lay abed, her long, dark hair draped over her shoulders, her once pretty face gaunt and flushed with fever. Her voice was abraded from her cough. April's sister, May, stood be-

1

side their mother's bed. A year younger than April, May's blue eyes were luminous with confusion, as were June's, who at ten, was curled tightly on the faded patchwork quilts against their mother's breast.

"Come here, sweet," Sarah beckoned to April.

April was slow to respond. If she took her time, warmed the cabin, perhaps her mother would fall asleep and wake up well again. But as if to discourage her hope, Sarah began to cough again. Spasms racked her thin, weakened body. She struggled to catch her breath.

April hurried across the cold wood floor to the bed where her mother lay. She helped lift her mother's head slightly so it was easier for her to inhale and watched Sarah draw air deep into her lungs. When she was at last stable again, Sarah smiled weakly and patted April's hand.

"There now," she said as April laid her back down on the pillow. "We'll begin now."

"Shouldn't you rest instead, Mama?" April protested. "We don't need a story tonight."

Sarah smiled again. "I'll rest soon. Just now it's important that I tell you a story. Your favorite story. The tale of the wildflowers."

"Mama," April continued to protest, "We know that one already. We don't need to hear it again."

"Ah, sweet." Sarah's drawn gaze rested on April and she managed to squeeze her hand. Her words were stilted. "Tonight the tale will change a bit. Tonight it will be even more special. Now listen.

"One very grand day, while God was creating our world, He decided to add beautiful flowers to the earth. The flowers, with help from the sweet rain and pure white snow, would come alive after a long winter and grow wild and free under the golden sun."

She closed her eyes, a peaceful smile on her lips. April was tense as she listened, but her mother seemed calm. Looked as if she could see clearly the words she was speaking in her mind's eye.

"Each flower was created sweetly fragrant and unique, and of different shapes and scents. And," Sarah took a stilting breath. "Because they were delicate and fragile, the flowers needed to be firmly planted so when a storm came they would survive."

April felt her heart lurch. Storm? She had never heard that part of the tale before.

"Then," Sarah continued with another weak smile, "Three little girls were born during the season of the wildflowers. Three beautiful sisters."

June and May giggled hesitantly.

April tried to smile but her apprehension made it difficult.

Sarah peered up at May and then April as she slid her thin hand over June's dark hair. Her tired eyes glistened. "The little girls' mama named them after the month in which they were born," she continued in her small voice. "She knew that like the flowers, they would be wild and thirsty and fragrant. They would grow by the river and make the land more beautiful. And with God watching over them, the little girls would be strong when the storms came."

"You said that again, Mama? That's the new part, isn't it?" May's voice cracked a bit. She grasped her mother's hand and held it tightly.

"Ah, but that's the special part," Sarah whispered soothingly. "The part I've been waiting for just the right moment to share with you. You see, outside a storm is raging, isn't it? The night is long and dark and the wind is fierce."

"Mama?" questioned May.

"And inside this cabin a different kind of storm is with us. The kind that is frightening and sad."

"I don't want to hear any more." June burrowed closer to her mother.

April watched her mother blink slowly, kiss June's head and try to squeeze May's hand with her limited strength.

"But you are strong and firmly planted, my wild-flowers," Sarah went on. "And you know that soon spring will come.

"June, my littlest flower."

June sniffed and refused to look up.

"I want you to promise me you will mind your sisters. You will try them greatly, dearest, but I know your heart. Listen and you will find a place for it."

April batted tears from her eyes.

"May, my angel."

A sob burst from May.

"Remember you are so precious and greatly valued. Do not hide from who you are, my sweet, and you will find your way."

April felt the knot in her throat tighten as her mother slowly turned her gaze to her.

"April." The word was barely a murmur.

"You need to rest now, Mama," April said gruffly. "I'll sing to you. Close your eyes."

"April." Sarah smiled. "How did I ever live before you came to me? You are truly the daughter of my heart. But oh, child, what a strong will you have. April, don't allow it to lead you astray."

April could only stare.

"Always remember. Always. And remember, my wildflowers. Your bloom will be most brilliant after the rain."

Chapter One

Late Fall, Colorado, 1867

April Wilde tapped her foot repeatedly against the dull hardwood floor. Those in the crowd watching her were sure to think she was enjoying the lively tune filling the air while a throng of dancers whirled and twirled around the temporary dance floor. She was, in fact, angrier than a bear with a bee sting, and would be more so if she had to leave her corner to search for June.

June knew April had an aversion to being at the dance in the first place. She knew April would hate it if she had to wind her way through the throng of townsfolk milling about in the Binghams' barn. Yet June had disappeared from the dance area nearly five minutes ago, along with her handsome dance partner. Leaving it up to April to find the little darling.

April silently fumed, her foot tapping away. Darn June anyway. She had promised to be extra good tonight while pleading to attend the Friday night Harvest Social. May hadn't helped when she'd explained how her new fiancé, Edwin Talbot, wanted her to attend. The glimmer of excitement in her sisters' eyes had been April's downfall.

Now she regretted it. She should be home canning the season's last batch of chokecherry jam. Instead she was at her first-ever town event, feeling as skittish as a filly, surrounded by people who'd just as soon see her leave, while music from banjos and fiddles filled the air and children giggled from the barn's high loft.

She had come to chaperone May and June, who were truly enjoying their evening. May was still twirling around the dance floor with Edwin, and June had danced with the multitude of men in the room as they scrambled for her attention.

A hush had fallen among the crowd when the three Wilde girls had entered the barn. Gazes continued to follow them with interest. It was rare for the sisters to attend a town event. Rarer still for April. She knew her presence was adding fresh fodder for the gossip mill. So she'd slid to a corner of the turned-out structure just after their arrival, intent on keeping a low profile. Now June was spoiling everything. Why had she ever agreed to attend—

As if to remind April of that very reason, May spun by on the arm of her husband-to-be, her pretty oval face flushed. Wearing the seafoam green dress the three girls had labored over for just such an occasion, the sight softened April. It was wonderful to see May smiling. There had been little enough pleasure for any of them during the past seven years of hardship. Now May had Edwin. She was going to marry him soon.

And if April read things right, June appeared to be just as taken by Luke Hart. Which was why the pair had been dancing together most of the night, and likely why they had disappeared together.

With a grudging sigh, April tucked a wayward lock of hair behind her ear, smoothed the bodice of her practical serge dress, and left the sanctuary of her corner.

She nodded politely as she edged by the Layburns, the missus known for the honey bees she raised, he for the whiskey he drank. As happened every Sunday at church, they pretended to ignore her and continued to sample from the plates of food in their hands. Sheriff Moss, on the other hand, acknowledged her passing with a tip of his head, but as usual his dark gaze followed April with suspicion, and his pregnant wife, Liv, lifted her chin a notch and turned away. Her northern neighbors, Clair and Stan Elliott, were more congenial than the others she'd known since she was a child, but they were too busy tending their passel of six kids to pay her any notice.

Not so Mrs. Claymore. The judge's wife—and most of her friends—had been glowering at April from across the barn all night, her plump lips pressed tightly together in disapproval.

April prayed for deliverance and continued to pay no heed to her adversary, just as she'd done for the past several years. She searched the room for June instead as the dancers shifted and people milled about.

"April!"

April's shoulders sagged in relief at the sound of June's merry voice. Pivoting, she saw her sister fanning her flushed face with her hand as she pressed her way through the crowd.

"It was so warm in here I decided to step outside

for some fresh air," she said with exuberance. "Isn't this the most wonderful dance?"

April could have argued otherwise but she held her tongue. She was more grateful for her younger sister's safe return than she was angry. "Where is Mr. Hart? Did you leave him outside?"

"Luke?" June shrugged as if Mr. Hart was old news. "I told him we'd danced enough. I think he was beginning to scare off the others." Still winded, she curled her arm in April's. "Come with me to get some lemonade. I'm absolutely parched."

April smiled with a small shake of her head. How she wished she had June's easygoing attitude. That she could flutter about, not worrying about a thing. She allowed June to pull her through the crowd to where several tables were set against the outer wall where the cows were normally stalled. The tables were laden with pies, cakes, lemonade, and cider bowls, and several women stood behind them serving the guests.

"Two lemonades, please," June called to one woman behind the table where they stopped. Her back to them, she was rearranging the plates of pie.

"Certainly, dear." She turned and reached for a tin and looked up with a warm smile, handing the lemonade to June. Then her gaze shifted to April and the smile faded. A look of censure replaced it, one April was familiar with. She watched the woman fold her arms over her chest.

"I believe I asked for *two* lemonades," June reminded her.

April glanced at her sister and saw June's pretty smile grow brighter, if possible. June passed April the tin in her hand.

"Please," June added to the woman.

The woman sighed and took another container, extending it to June.

"Thank you," April said politely. Then she took June's arm and stepped away from the table.

"Ohhh, sometimes . . ." June whispered. "That's Yolanda Pierce. Everyone knows she and Sadie Claymore are like this." She curled her index finger around another.

"Don't worry about it," April soothed, determined not to let the woman spoil June's night. "You know I'm used to their resentment. But thank you for standing up to her."

"Yes, well . . ."

April smiled. "Look, there's May. She and Edwin look nice dancing together, don't they?"

June waved, the woman behind the table forgotten. Which was what April wanted. May and June were sensitive to April's rejection, but because her sisters had also been socializing with the other settlers in the area for several months now, April was doing her best to distance them from her own troubles. So far it was working.

"April! June!"

May danced to a stop in front of her sisters, Edwin Talbot with her. "You don't mind if we take a break, do you, Edwin?" she asked her fiancé. Winded, she fanned her face.

Edwin smiled weakly. "If you'd like. Although it is rather impolite to stop in the middle of a tune. Sam Collins is a bank customer. I wouldn't want him to think I disliked his fiddle playing."

May looked at April as if hoping she had a response.

"I'm sure Mr. Collins won't take offense," April said.

May smiled. "Of course not, Edwin. We've danced the last three dances and he's played every one."

"But we danced the four previous ones to Lawson Dike's fiddle. Sam might remember. But if you need to rest . . ."

"No. No. I wouldn't want Mr. Collins to be upset. If you think we should finish the dance we will."

"Mr. Talbot can explain to Mr. Collins later," April offered.

May sighed in relief. "Yes, that's the answer. Thank you for the suggestion, April. I am rather tired."

April forced a smile at the medium-sized bank manager May was engaged to marry, even though he didn't look pleased. She still couldn't help wonder, as she did many times, what May saw in Edwin. Especially at times like this when he seemed to make a mountain out of a molehill. But he was highly respected in the community, and just establishing the new bank. He'd offer May a good, stable life. April was thankful for that.

"We just got some lemonade, May," June beamed. "It's delicious. I was just as worn out as you look."

"We already had a glass," Edwin replied.

"From the table where Mrs. Philips is at," May added. "It was very sour, but Edwin is afraid if we go to the table Miss Pierce is at, Mrs. Philips will be offended."

Oh, goodness, April said to herself.

"Perhaps Mrs. Philips will leave her post soon. Then we'll get another drink." His words punctuated, Edwin tugged on the sleeves of his seersucker suit before smoothing his normally impeccably combed hair back where the strands had fallen onto his shiny forehead.

"Isn't this the most fun?" June asked then, shifting topics.

May nodded. "I wonder what the Binghams did with all their animals. We'd never be able to empty our barn and make it look this clean."

"We should have come to last year's Harvest Social," June expounded. "And the one before that."

Something inside April twisted near her heart, even though she knew June meant no harm by her words.

"No, no, June." May's blue gaze locked with April's, her eyes sympathetic. "It was important we stay away, remember? We had no choice."

"Yes, of course," June agreed. Again she took April's arm in hers. "I was just caught up in the moment. It's easy to forget our troubles on a night like tonight, isn't it, April?"

April wished she felt the same as June. Nothing about tonight was easy for the eldest Wilde sister. Or made her forget the troubles that had followed them since their mother's death so long ago. If anything, the way she continued to be spurned made her difficulties more prominent. But she squeezed her sister's hand, not willing to shatter June's perception. "I'm glad you've had such a wonderful time, but we really need to leave soon. It must be close to midnight and we have a long trip home."

"Oh April, one more dance, please!" June peered at April with such childlike longing April knew she couldn't deny her request. The seventeen-year-old beauty looked as stunning tonight as April had ever seen her. May had arranged June's dark hair by pulling it away from her exuberant face, clasping it with combs at the crown of her head and letting it dangle in fine wisps about her neck and temples. The satin blue gown they had all stitched, enhanced June's trim figure and beautiful face.

"One more," April told her and was rewarded with an excited hug, before June suddenly went still.

"B-but I can't ask anyone to dance. That would be outrageous!"

"Where's Tobias Reeves and John Simpson? Or did they get tired of waiting for you to quit dancing with Luke Hart?" May teased. When June failed to see the humor in her words, she added, "Oh, don't fret, you can dance with Edwin. That should soothe Mr. Collins, and I've danced enough." May turned to her fiancé, her smile straining a little as she stared at him. Brushing a wisp of her pale blond hair from her face she added, "Is that all right with you, Edwin? That will solve any problem we've caused."

"Oh, would you, Mr. Talbot?" June burst out. Then, as if remembering herself, she calmed. "I mean, if, that is . . ."

"I'd be happy to escort you to the dance floor, Miss June." Edwin's smile was as lukewarm as his hair and his pale brown eyes. He added to May and April, "I only hope no one starts a rumor about this. I'd lose my job if scandal broke."

June failed to hear him. She bounced in place excitedly. May lost her smile but stepped away from Edwin's side so he could extend his arm to June. Soon the pair were pressing into the throng of dancers and disappearing, leaving May and April to watch.

May slid closer to her sister. "I don't understand him sometimes," she sighed. "Was I wrong to stop dancing? Wrong to ask him to dance with June?"

"I would have done the same thing," April told her. She brushed May's arm. "Mr. Talbot will come around." She only hoped she was right.

She saw her sister smile again, before it faded altogether and she glanced at April. "You're miserable, aren't you?"

"Don't worry about me. I'm fine," April fibbed. She couldn't wait to leave the noisy, overwarm barn.

"You can't fool me." Only a year apart, May and April had an awareness between the two of them June didn't share.

"Well, a bit," April reluctantly admitted.

May faced her. "You haven't had any fun at all?"

April shrugged noncommittally.

"I saw a man ask you to dance."

April scrunched her nose. "You know I wouldn't dance with Cirrus Claymore if he offered me a hundred horses."

"Not Cirrus. Did he try again? No, Mr. Moore."

April dropped her gaze. "I declined. Besides, I can't dance."

"You can dance as well as me and June," May rebutted. "Mama taught us all how and you know it. June and I haven't forgotten how. You just don't want to dance."

"I've chosen to forget, thank you." April lifted her head again and tilted it slightly. "But I'm thrilled you and June have had a good time."

"It would've been nicer if Edwin wasn't so worried. And if you'd shared in the fun. I'll make certain you enjoy the next dance we attend."

There would never be another dance, April vowed. Her head was throbbing. She was weary from smiling false smiles and dodging scornful glares. All she wanted to do was go home to the small cabin she shared with her sisters, where she was safe.

As if in answer to her prayer the music finally faded, everyone applauded and June and Edwin returned. April quickly slid out the door while her sisters said their good-byes. A few minutes later they were seated atop their buckboard, bundled against the chill for the ride home. June and May continued to reminisce about the evening, while April finally felt her tension begin to diminish. She clucked at the pair of horses, Solomon and Samson, and directed them down the road winding along the South Platte River, while basking in the tranquility of the calm, cool October night.

But as her sisters chattered on excitedly, April began to wonder how different their lives would have been had their father not abandoned them. Clearly, their mother wouldn't have died from a broken heart seven years earlier. And if that event hadn't occurred, tonight wouldn't have been the girls' first social occasion, because April would have never earned the wrath of Sadie Claymore.

The cold air whipped through April's hair and overcoat as she solemnly pondered. Then she reminded herself that it was fruitless to dwell on things she couldn't change. Besides, now that all was said and done, she was proud of the vibrant young women her sisters had become. May could have done worse than the manager of the First Bank of Colorado. And June and Luke Hart would make a good match. Luke was handsome, strong, and a respected blacksmith in the booming settlement of Ruley. April wouldn't be surprised if both girls were married within a year.

Though the thought was a staggering one, it also gave April a little thrill. She would hate to see her sisters marry and move away, but once they did April would be able to pursue her own dream. Her father might have deserted the family but he'd left them a hundred acres of prime land along the South Platte northwest of Ruley. The land was just right for the herd of beautiful horses April wanted to breed and

raise. So far making ends meet had prevented her from
buying a mare for Solomon so she could breed stock
for the army and cattle operations that were starting
up all over. But if May and June married that could
all change. April would save every cent she could
from selling chokecherry jam to Mr. Dortch at the
mercantile and from eating less and mending more.
She'd buy Solomon the best mare she could find and
somehow lasso the wild sorrel she'd see running with
the mustangs. She'd have two mares to work with and
her business would begin.

She looked heavenward, put at ease by the sight of
the night sky lightened by a full moon and a dome of
brilliant stars. She could almost sense her mother smiling down upon her and couldn't help but wonder if,
after seven long years, she was finally going to see
the spring her mother promised just before her death.

She was ready for the storm to end. But, like always, she was afraid that was too much to pray for.

She shook herself from her musings, and as if to
remind her that real winter loomed, a gust of cold wind
ruffled her hair. Then the farm emerged from the darkness and as she steered Solomon and Samson toward
the barn they suddenly whinnied and shied.

And a cow in the barn mooed in distress.

April brought the wagon to an abrupt halt. Her heart
thumped frantically in her chest. "Shhh," she admonished the giggling girls when they failed to hear the
signs of danger.

May and June instantly quieted. Having lived alone
since their mother's death, far from neighbors or town,
they had battled harsh weather, the angry Arapahoe,
wild animals and famine. Danger was real to them.

"What is it?" May whispered.

"Someone's in the barn."

Solomon blew again in confirmation.

April lifted the rifle beside her while May and June grabbed theirs from the wagon bed. Slowly, quietly, the three girls dropped from the buckboard to the ground. April glanced around but the night was dark. Still, seeing no one in the shadows, she motioned her sisters to circle the barn. She circled it from the opposite direction. Just when she reached the wide, closed door, she heard rustling again and a muffled complaint.

The intruder was male, she determined by his voice. And not Indian unless he was an Indian with a southern accent. She prayed there was only one. When May and June were in place near the far side of the barn door, April slowly and quietly pushed it open to reveal a man unsaddling his horse. In the light generated from the barn's lantern she could see that he was tall and dressed in a fitted red wool shirt, faded blue trousers and black leather boots. His wide-brimmed hat sat on his horse's rump.

His broad back to them as he unbuckled the cinch gave April the opportunity to move to the center of the open door. May and June moved in behind her, and then April cocked her gun.

She waited silently as the man froze in place, then slowly turned to face her, his hands spread wide and high. He was even broader than she first noticed, the wool fabric of his shirt stretched tautly over his muscles as he kept his arms lifted high. She blinked when she saw his handsome features; his windblown light brown hair that shimmered in the glow of the lantern, his cobalt gaze that was sweeping over her from head to toe before finally settling on her own, and his thick brown brows drawing together in a steeped V.

"Evening," he said in a cautious southern baritone. He tipped his head slightly in greeting.

Her heart skipped a beat, before racing on. His even, slow drawl made her insides melt. She had to force herself to concentrate on the feel of the cold, unforgiving rifle in her hands. "Good evening," she replied. She realized her voice was too high-pitched and prayed she hadn't betrayed her nervousness. Determined to concentrate, she glanced sharply around the barn, trying to see if anything was out of order, if he'd been stealing anything. Noting nothing unusual she fixed her gaze on him again, then realized that wasn't the smartest thing to do. She found herself almost drowning in the depths of his eyes. "You want to tell me what you're doing in our barn?"

The man cleared his throat. "I went to the house. Looking for someone. No one was home," he said simply.

When she remained silent, he continued. "It's late, and I was tired." He extended his arms further, as if to encompass the interior of the barn. "So I thought I'd get some rest out here and return to the house, see if there was anyone home in the morning."

"Why?" April asked him. Her finger on her gun's hammer, she held the weapon tight, more to stop her hands from shaking than anything else. And to stop her from being distracted. It was hard to think of him as dangerous. He certainly didn't fit the profile of a grizzled train robber or cattle thief. His speech was much too refined, *he* was much too handsome. She had the strongest desire to stare at him.

She fought off the sensation. "Why?" she asked again. "Who are you looking for? What do you want?"

"Why?" he repeated her question, then shifted his weight from one booted foot to the other. "It is pretty late. Maybe we should wait to talk about that until morning like I was planning. You look rather tired yourself."

April wasn't about to wait. Did he think she was going to be able to sleep while he stayed in the barn? She notched her chin. "You don't really think I'm going to agree to that, do you, mister? Now is just fine, I think. If my sisters and I are to get any sleep it'll be after your departure. And you're right, it's late. We wouldn't want to delay it."

The man briefly eyed May and June behind her, as if seeing them for the first time. But they too, had their guns trained on him. "Yes, well . . ." His gaze darkened somewhat. "I was hoping, that is, I wasn't planning on leaving. Are you three the only people who live here?"

April lifted the barrel of the rifle, which, she could see, succeeded in making him narrow his eyes in irritation. "I'd rethink my plans, mister, if I were you. And rethink asking any questions before you explain who you are and what you're doing here. Soon. As you noted, we are tired," she told him. "And low on patience."

The solid line of his jaw tightened. "Where can I find Mrs. Wilde?"

His words stung April's heart. She squared her shoulders. "Who wants to know?"

"I have a piece of paper," he said instead. He started to turn toward his saddlebags, thought better of it. "May I get it out? Since you're determined to do this now, it will explain."

A piece of paper? Explain? She wanted to ask him what he meant, but didn't want to reveal any undo concern. "That's not necessary," she countered. "I'm not interested in your explanation. All I'm interested in is you getting back on your horse and riding out of here. Now, thank you."

Her words seemed to have no impact. He merely raked his hand through his hair, a fleeting half-smile crossing his lips. "Miss whoever-you-are, I can't oblige you. I have a written statement here that tells me I don't have to. Interested now?"

The rifle grew slippery in April's clammy hands. Her legs weakened with sudden trepidation. Gone was the fluttery feeling she'd had when she first saw him. She knew now he was very dangerous.

"Maybe we should look at the paper, April," June whispered from behind her.

April thrust the gun forward an inch. "Who are you?"

"Did I hear you call her April?" the man said to June. "Did she call you April?" he repeated, his attention back on April. "April Wilde? And did you say you were sisters?"

"Who are you?" she prodded again, this time jamming the gun barrel forward several inches.

The man grumbled. "Will Caulder. Originally from Virginia. More recently, Cripple Creek."

"Cripple Creek!" June took a step and lowered her gun. "Do you know our father then? Have you seen him? Is he coming home? Is that why you're here?"

"June!" May admonished and lifted the barrel of June's gun toward Caulder again.

"Oh, dear." June backed up a pace and took firm hold of the weapon, remorse written on her face.

"Well?" April asked. She prayed he couldn't hear the catch in her throat. "Do you know our father?"

The man stood in place, as if stunned. He glanced from May to June to April. "Yes and no," he sighed.

His answer made April's irritation rise. She was

weary of the sparring with this man. She could tell he was confused at discovering who she was, who her sisters were, but she was just as confused as to why, and why this southerner was standing in her barn. Tightening her finger hold on the barrel, she edged it close to her eye. "You've got one minute to explain, mister, or be on your horse and gone. Do you know our father or not?"

"I *knew* your father." He paused, as if in thought, then turned slightly to pet his horse. For the first time he didn't look April in the eye. "Justus Wilde is dead."

June gasped and burst into tears. May gasped too, and put her arm around the younger girl.

April didn't even blink. Justus Wilde had died a long time ago as far as she was concerned. "What does *he* have to do with *you*?" she went on. She wasn't at all sure she wanted to hear what he had to say, but she knew it was necessary. "Well?" she pressed when he was too slow to respond.

He finally faced her again, his gaze piercing, his stance rigid. "Look, Miss Wilde. I thought you and your sisters were little girls. I could have sworn that's what I was told. But I suppose that's irrelevant now. What is relevant is that your father, Justus Wilde, made me the owner of this property." He eyed her sharply. "And I've come to claim it."

"What?" June and May exclaimed together.

April's heart skipped a beat, then plunged to her stomach. How could she have thought this man wasn't dangerous?

"I have proof," he went on. He took a step backward, continuing to keep an eye on April's gun as he pointed to his saddlebags. "I wasn't expecting it to be like this. I mean, I thought I'd tell your mother. That

is, I was going to break it to her in a better way. And
then help you, you all, move on, but—"

June sobbed louder. She turned into May's arms,
dropping her rifle into the hay.

"It's time for you to leave, Mr. Caulder," April all
but snarled. She jabbed her rifle forward again.

Will Caulder froze.

"Now. Ruley's only two miles from here." Her gaze
still on him, April bent down, retrieved June's dis-
carded gun and pointed it at the man also. "You've
got to the count of three. After that you'll still be making your journey, but in a good deal of pain."

He continued to stand where he was despite her
threats. It was obvious he didn't believe her, which
made April fume inwardly. She wasn't a child, *and*
she didn't make idle threats.

The boom was deafening. Every living thing in the
barn jumped, June and May screamed, and Will Caulder's horse shrieked and bolted for the door. Chickens
and roosters squawked and scattered, and the cows
began bucking against their wooded stalls.

Even April jerked from the gun's recoil, while
Caulder ducked first, then whirled his head to glare at
her.

"What do you think you're doing?" he shouted. His
long-legged stride brought him forward before she
could react. He halted in front of her and grabbed
June's gun from her hand. He quickly tossed it to the
ground and tried to grab the rifle April had fired into
the roof.

April swiveled the gun around and hit him in the
shoulder with the butt. He stumbled slightly, but regained his balance just as May jumped on his back.
With a grunt as she pummeled his back with her fists,
he rolled to one side and deposited her onto the hay-

filled ground. Then he turned to see June try to lasso him with a rope. He dodged the rope, grabbed it and sent June, with a cry, tumbling next to May.

When he recovered again he eyed April with undisguised exasperation. "That was the most ridiculous thing I've seen a female do yet," he growled, taking a step toward her. "What on God's green earth did you think you'd accomplish by shooting a hole in the roof and spooking every living thing in sight?"

April backed up a pace but continued to hold the gun like a broom, ready to wallop him. "Be glad that bullet was planted skyward instead of through your heart," she replied.

"If you think a silly shot from a gun held by a silly female is going to scare me off, you're wrong, lady." He lunged, catching April around the waist. She groaned as the rifle went flying from her hands, and his body landed on top of hers in the padded hay.

Furious, she immediately pushed at him. But he grabbed her arms and pinned her beneath him. When she could do nothing but uselessly push at him and move her head from side to side, he glared at her.

"Don't make this any more difficult than it already is," he told her. He checked to see that May and June were still struggling to their feet. "I didn't like coming here this way. I hadn't planned on telling Wilde's daughters this property is mine. But it's the truth and I need it. I was hoping your mother would be a reasonable person, so we could maybe come to some kind of agreement or settlement, or understanding."

"If you think," April ground out, "that I'm going to just accept your word as proof that my home is now your home, you're out of your mind, Mr. Caulder. I've worked too long, too hard—" She briefly closed her eyes, envisioning for one second what would happen if he was telling the truth. What would they do? Where would they go? All April's dreams . . . All her hopes, would vanish. And after everything she had been through?

No. Please, no.

This could not be happening.

April growled and bucked. The intruder didn't budge an inch. In exasperation she let her body go slack. Strangely, he relaxed his hold the moment she did. She glared up at him, struck again by his handsomeness, and felt a slow shiver work its way up her arms, across her shoulders and down her back. She cursed her own betrayal, wondering how she could still find the man attractive after his announcement, after his attack.

"Ready to hear me out?" he asked as if he thought she had suddenly come to her senses.

She began to rebut him, determined to tell him just what she really thought, when, from the corner of her eye April saw May slowly approaching them, a wicked-looking shovel raised above her head.

April smiled. "Not on your life." A moment later her sister brought the shovel down on top of Will Caulder's crown. April watched as he stared at her in confusion, then promptly fell to one side.

Pushing away any misguided guilt, April slid out from beneath him with a grunt. "That'll teach you."

"I hope I didn't hurt him too badly," May worried, discarding the shovel.

April frowned at her sister for her generosity.

"Here, help me tie him up." June shakily handed May some rope.

"Double knot everything," April told them both and watched them do just that. She felt the tension in her frame begin to ease now that the immediacy of the threat he posed was over.

"What are we going to do with him?" May asked, concern still evident in her voice.

April crossed her arms, satisfied as she stared at the unconscious intruder. "Well, he wanted a good night's rest," she said. "He's going to get his wish."

Chapter Two

Will's eyes opened slowly. He blinked against an
uncomfortable throbbing coursing through his head.
He heard his own groan as he tried to move his hand
to rub the spot that ached so much, only to find he
couldn't budge.

That brought his eyes open wider. And brought
more pain. He squinted. Sunlight filtered in through
woodpecker holes and warped wall board, revealing
his stale surroundings. He found he was lying on a
pile of itchy hay in one corner of the barn. A rooster
waddled by not five feet in front of him, while milk
cows peered at him from over the doors of their stalls.

His gaze continued to travel, landing on wood and
framing, farm implements, a buckboard, a big bay
grazing in another stall, his own black beside it, and
finally on the young woman dozing in a chair propped
against the barn door. Dressed in a simple brown dress

with just a bit of white lace around the collar, she had an old blanket around her shoulders and a rifle sitting in her lap.

April Wilde.

He swallowed hard, remembering their meeting with vivid detail now. How his heart had lurched when first he saw her. He hadn't had a clue who she was. Justus Wilde was an older man; he knew she couldn't be his wife. And yet he'd never given a thought to the fact that Wilde's "girls" weren't just that: young girls, not grown women. Nor that *this* daughter would be one of such a striking beauty, with haunting green eyes that spoke of past hardship and fierce—proven— determination. Had she really bested him? The ropes binding him confirmed she had.

Lyonel Simms had misled him. Wilde's partner had told Will Wilde's daughters were in the care of their mother.

April Wilde was no child.

At the moment she was peaceful in repose. She looked like an angel with smooth skin and gold-spun hair. But Will wasn't fooled. There was a wildcat beneath her halo. And she was obviously the ringleader of her band of sisters.

He grimaced, tried to shift position again and found himself trussed up tighter than a sack of flour.

"Hey!" he shouted, instantly regretting it. He gritted his teeth as waves of pain shot through his head.

But his raised voice did the trick. April Wilde's eyes flew open. She stared right at him, through him for a brief moment, before her senses caught up to her. Then her green gaze settled on him with clarity. She pursed her soft red lips and narrowed her eyes, the white of them shot through with tiny veins of red that spoke of her fatigue but didn't diminish the sparkling green.

"Are you going to keep me tied up like this forever?" His tone was as harsh as he could make it with his head pounding. He wasn't about to let her get away with besting him. He needed to establish that right away.

In answer, she slowly rolled her shoulders and stood up, the blanket falling to the ground behind her. The gun she'd fired into the roof was still in her hand. He guessed she'd slept in the chair all night. But her lack of sleep failed to steal away her beauty. "For as long as it takes." She covered her yawn with her hand.

"As long as it takes to keep me from claiming what's mine?" he asked, more to take his mind off his last thought than anything else. "Look in my saddlebag then. The proof is there."

She brushed stray strands of soft curls from her cream-hued face and continued to stare at him. "As long as it takes for May to fetch the sheriff so he can haul you out of here."

Will lifted a brow, surprised by her statement. "Go right ahead and fetch the sheriff. It will only prove what I've told you. I own this place and I have a right to it. I'm here to stay."

He watched her complexion pale and the urge to snatch his words back stung his mind. The last thing he'd meant to do last night was start off on the wrong foot. He had assumed he'd reach the farm and find Justus Wilde's wife and three "girls." He'd calmly relieve them of the burden of the farm, then help them get to another relative or town. He pictured them being grateful, wanting to leave the harsh west. Pictured them heading back east where they belonged.

He certainly hadn't meant to find April Wilde all

grown up, or to spring the news on her like she'd forced him to do. But the woman had rubbed him thinner than the blade on his knife. And forced him to retaliate. "I might go for the sheriff myself. Tell him just what you ladies did to me last night. I think there's a law against holding someone against their will."

"As there is for lying, forgery . . . murder."

"Murder?" Will struggled with the ropes that bound him. Was she serious? He wasn't about to take a chance and find out. "I didn't murder your father. Or lie, or forge anything. I won this place in a legitimate card game, fair and square."

She had turned away, and walked over to pet the big bay he'd noticed and admired. Now she faced him again, suddenly attentive. She obviously knew her father was a gambler. He could tell she wasn't pleased.

"I have witnesses," he added. "Two. They signed the document."

She began to chew her bottom lip. For a moment he thought she might cry, her pretty green eyes grew so luminous. Then she lifted her chin in an obvious display of defiance. "Witnesses, Mr. Caulder? Or other gamblers you paid for their signatures?"

He grumbled. He ached, needed to shift position, and he was furious at being outdone by three small-boned females.

But as long as he was bound tighter than a braid of horse hair, Will was at her mercy. All he could do was stare at her with undisguised irritation, appeal to her conscience.

She startled him when after a few moments she shoved the rifle against the horse stall, took a knife from one of several pegs on the wall, and walked over to him. It flashed through his mind than instead of gaining an appeal, he had gained a sentence; she was going to slice his throat. But she grabbed his hands that were tied behind his back and began to cut through the rope.

"Show me," she nearly shouted then, her voice cracking. "Find the disgraceful deed you've been boasting about and show it to me."

Will felt the rope give. His muscles and joints protested as they found their freedom. With a stifled groan he sat up, working the kinks from his bones, and got to his feet. All the while he watched April Wilde standing poised for his document.

For a full minute he couldn't take his eyes off her. He stood there looking dumb instead of providing her the evidence she requested. It struck him he should ride back to Cripple Creek and ask Lyonel Simms a few questions. Like why Wilde had gambled away his daughters' land. Like why Will had been led to believe the daughters were young girls.

But then he buried his misgivings, ignoring the pain thrumming through his head as well. This place was his future, his family's future. The Caulders had lost everything in the War Between the States, and Will had been searching for a new life ever since. One that would satisfy his soul and rescue his family. For two years he'd traveled the west, trying to earn enough money to begin again. He'd laid railroad until his hands bled, worked cattle till a stampede nearly wiped out the herd, and acted as a scout for a wagon train that saw more death to sickness than he'd seen in the war. Which was considerable.

It was tales of gold—and ultimately fate—Will decided, that led him over Pike's Peak from Colorado Springs to Cripple Creek. And a card game with Justus Wilde.

A hundred-acre farm was his reward. He'd already

wired his parents and sister, detailing his windfall.
They were on their way from his Uncle Henry's home
in Jefferson City, Tennessee, where they'd refuged
since the war. He knew they'd love the lush basin at
the brim of the Rocky Mountains where his new farm
sat. And Will wasn't about to let anything change that.
Especially April Wilde. He couldn't.

Walking to the stall where his horse stood, he
peered over the side to see his saddlebags on the
ground. He glanced back at April, wondering why she
hadn't pilfered through his belongings while he was
unconscious and found the document herself. She
could've easily destroyed it. Put an end to his claim.

But she obviously hadn't done so, because she continued to wait for him, her arms crossed, a look of
desperation and defiance and possibly hope that she
could prove him a fraud written on her face, so he
stepped through the stall door and reached straight for
the pouch that held his future. Extracting the parch-
ment, he unfolded it, reread the print and gave another
prayer of thanks. He still found himself a little stunned
over the windfall.

Without a word he returned to her and held out the
deed. She scanned the document for a long time before
her face and hands paled, the green of her eyes
dimmed. When her hands suddenly began to shake she
thrust the paper into Will's chest.

"It might still be a forgery," she announced.

"It might be." He had to grant her that much.

"You could have held a gun to my father's head
and made him sign it."

"I could have." He calmly folded the document.
"But I didn't, Miss Wilde. I won it. And in my book
that means it's mine. Granted, it's not the best way to

gain something. But I've worked hard at other things that have never brought me anything but heartache."

She stared up at him with those big eyes of hers and he felt himself melting inside.

"What do you want?" she asked.

He considered her question. While in the bustling mining town of Cripple Creek the answer had been clear. Now standing a foot in front of Justus Wilde's daughter it was anything but clear. "I need a home. For my family. My parents and sister," he finally said. "That's why I came here."

"And *my* sisters and I?"

Will didn't have an answer. "I wasn't expecting you. I mean, Lyonel Sims told me you and your sisters were little girls. He thought you were still living with your mother and would jump at the chance to go back east."

"Well as you can see we're not little girls, Mr. Caulder."

She didn't need to tell Will so. "And your mother?" He already thought he knew the answer but had to ask anyway.

"And our mother is dead," she confirmed.

He nodded, but when he didn't say anything else— didn't know what else to say—she walked from the barn with her head high. Will followed her as far as the barn door. There he paused and, in the daylight, watched her trek across dirt and dormant autumn grass toward the small cabin he'd seen only in a dark silhouette last night. She climbed two porch steps and entered the cabin, closing the front door behind her.

Will leaned against the barn door, feeling the aged wood creak and splinter beneath him as his chest tightened and his conscience challenged him. How'd something so simple turn into such a mess? Why had the farm been dropped into his lap, only to turn so complicated now? He wished he knew.

With an exhale of air, Will decided April Wilde was just going to have to understand that he needed this place more than she did.

April halted just inside the cabin door, shivering. The document couldn't be real. *It couldn't be*, she prayed. But she was well aware that her father, on top of everything else, was a notorious gambler. He could very well have wagered his daughters' home away. And, in April's opinion, never thought twice about it.

Her mother would have defended Justus Wilde, made excuses for him and painted a prettier picture, but April lived every day knowing her father's weaknesses were the cause of her mother's death. She'd clung to the hope that one day she'd have the opportunity to confront him, tell him exactly how much she despised him, and finally seek justice for her mother's suffering, but, it seemed, even that had been stripped away from her now that he was dead.

And still reaching from the grave to harm his family, if Caulder's claim was real. How the man—or anyone for that matter—could try to collect on such a vulgar wager, she couldn't fathom. And yet she didn't know what she could do about it. How she could stop him.

"April?"

April's attention was drawn to May standing in the doorway of the bedroom she shared with June. Still in her heavy wool nightdress, May's face was flushed and puffy from recent sleep, her blond hair tangled. "You were supposed to wake me and June hours ago so we could take our turn watching Mr. Caulder," she said.

April forced a smile. "I know, but Mr. Caulder was still unconscious so I decided to let you both sleep." She grabbed her coat from a peg behind the door, shoved her arms into the sleeves, and headed for the kitchen, where she pulled down a water bucket.

May remained in the doorway. June shuffled up behind her, yawning. "What's going on?" she asked. "It's after dawn." Her eyes widened and the fog of sleep departed. "April, why didn't you wake us? Is that awful man still in the barn?"

"She stayed with him," May answered for April.

"It wasn't any trouble," April assured them.

"But you must have been cold."

"And uncomfortable."

"I was fine, until a few minutes ago when he woke up." April nodded toward the door with a frown. "He's still in the barn. At least he was."

"What do you mean was?" June asked frantically.

"I untied him."

"You untied him?" May's eyes widened.

April chewed on her bottom lip, silently admonishing herself for doing such a foolish thing. It was just that in the daylight he hadn't seemed nearly as dangerous. And she'd been so angry with him for acting as if *she* were wrong. She was still angry. With the entire situation. He had a black soul if he could ride in and claim ownership of her property without regard to how it would affect her and her sisters.

"Oh April, I'm so sorry I forgot to hold my gun on him last night." June took a step forward. "When he said he'd been in Cripple Creek, why I . . . I hoped he had a message from . . . well, I'm sorry."

"June dear, don't scold yourself."

"I was very foolish. I could have brought us all harm. Why don't I think before I act?"

April reached for her sister's hand. "Because you're young. Stop fretting."

"We need to think about what we're going to do now." May fondled June's long flowing hair. "And not worry about last night."

"May," April said then. She moved back a pace. "I want you to take Solomon and head for Ruley. Since Sheriff Moss was in town for the dance last night, hopefully he's still there. Bring him back with you. Tell him there's a strange man on our property and he refuses to leave. Moss will have to return with you. June and I will do your morning chores so you can leave right away. The sooner you return with the sheriff the sooner Mr. Caulder will be gone."

"All right," May replied. "That's exactly what we need to do." She brightened. "I'll get ready just as fast as I can."

"Is he going to kick us out if the sheriff won't make him leave?" June wanted to know. She sniffed and smoothed her dark hair from her face. April noticed the tears in her eyes.

April blinked rapidly herself. "Not if we can help it," she stated firmly. She'd never let him. "We'll have to come up with another idea if the sheriff won't help us." She forced another smile. Her sisters had always looked to her for comfort, for advice, and for assurance. She wasn't about to fail them now. "Mr. Caulder is just a nuisance who's been sent here to plague us. We'll deal with him just like we've dealt with everything else that's come our way. Won't we?"

"Yes!" June shouted enthusiastically.

"Yes!" May added with the same fervor.

April wished she felt as confident. But she'd never let them know before that confidence eluded her, and she wasn't about to start now. "I'm going down to the river. June, start breakfast, please. We don't want our May to leave on an empty stomach."

She stepped back outside, bucket in hand, determined not to let this latest ordeal get the best of her. Will Caulder and his claim would somehow vanish. Until then it was just an inconvenience, just another in a long list. She'd gotten through all the rest. She'd get through this one, too.

She pulled the door closed behind her and abruptly stopped when she saw the man of her thoughts sitting on the porch step. His chin was resting in his hand and he was looking west at the Rockies. *Her* Rockies. *Her mountains.* The house sat on a ridge above the Platte and provided a spectacular western view of the formidable peaks. It was the one thing her father had done right, this farm, and April had spent long hours staring across the expanse, enjoying the ever-changing layers and colors and awesome beauty.

Now though, her heart took an unexpected eager leap at the sight of Will Caulder's broad back, even though she was once again angered by his presence. She reasoned her inner workings kept betraying her because there had never been a man in her barn, or one sitting on her porch. The only men who had ever visited the farm were the circuit sheriff, Moss, when he occasionally passed by, Stan Elliott the time his middle son had gone missing, and Cirrus Claymore— repeatedly—and he didn't count.

Caulder was different, even if he shouldn't have been different enough to make her react so strangely. April felt intimidated by his southern upbringing, his cultured dialect. His surety that he'd won their battle. She also couldn't get over, even though she wanted to, his handsomeness. The way his light brown hair blew slightly at the edge of his shirt's collar made her swallow tightly.

He was a villain, she reminded herself.

Her hands clenched around the bucket handle and she took a step forward, determined to ignore and go around him.

"Miss Wilde." Her name rolled from his tongue. "We haven't concluded our business." His back was to her still. She was jolted to find he knew she was behind him, and more so by his distasteful words. Business? Conclusion?

He made it easier to latch on to her anger again. "There won't be any conclusion to this *business* for awhile, Mr. Caulder," she growled. She picked up her pace, brushed past him and down the stairs.

The early morning cold stung her cheeks, the crisp air tinged with the scent of the new season. April pulled her coat more securely around her frame, and trudged down the rolling, sloping plains toward the river. The Platte meandered along the midsection of the hundred acres the Wildes had homesteaded when April was seven. The river added to the land's charm as it circled and weaved and ran its course. More importantly, the river provided the girls with the water they needed.

She felt Caulder's gaze burning into her back as she walked away from the house. She wasn't about to turn around to see if he was really watching her, but she did hurry until she made it to the copse of shedding chokecherry bushes and oak scrub that lined the bank. She darted into the thicket to escape his view. Then, feeling more at ease, April walked to the water's edge and sat down on a fallen tree limb, sighing heavily.

She wasn't very confident that Sheriff Moss would help much, even though she was sending May to fetch him. She'd done so just so her sisters would think April knew what she was doing. There was a small chance Caulder would be forced to leave. But small at best. April's real strategy was to gain a few more hours to come up with a better way to fight him. The truth was, Sheriff Moss would most likely side with the interloper. Even though he was supposed to protect the citizens of the area, he was male. And Sadie Claymore had hardened Moss toward April just like she had the rest of the settlers in and around Ruley. She knew he wouldn't stand in Caulder's way if he didn't have to. Which meant April was on her own, as usual. It would be up to her to do something else. But what, short of murdering Caulder and hiding his body? No one would ever know except May and June, and . . . God. Her own conscience was already rebelling for just thinking such a thing. And she could hear her mother's voice loud and clear, scolding her first and then reminding her to have faith. Reminding her of all the times April had thought she would never make it through the day, only to find strength and determination and a path. Surely the same would happen again. But her thoughts verified how desperate she felt.

She lifted her chin. She had no intention of doing evil for evil. Surely Will Caulder wouldn't get away with his treachery.

As the river meandered downstream, April felt her tension diminish a bit. All would be well. She just had to have faith. She closed her eyes, praying Will Caulder would go away.

"It sure is taking you a long time to fill one bucket of water."

Her tranquility collapsing, April jumped off the tree limb and spun around to see Will Caulder in all his arrogance standing only feet away. Her tension returned full force, her heart sped up, her hands grew clammy, and her blood rushed faster through her veins. She stared at the intruder with renewed resentment burning in her sea-green eyes. "You are a vile person, Mr. Caulder," she ground out through clenched teeth. "Do you always sneak up on people just for the thrill of it? Intentionally startling them? Are you trying to frighten me to death so you can have my home?"

He had his hat on now. It was the first time April had seen him in the sleek felt, and of course, the look only added to his handsome appeal. He tipped it forward a bit, rakishly, and rubbed his temple. "I thought perhaps you'd fallen into the water, Miss Wilde," he countered smoothly. "I was merely doing the neighborly thing by looking out for your welfare."

"That is hardly likely," she fumed. "I've lived here all my life. I know the river. And if I had, for some strange reason, fallen in, I think you would have heard my cry for help." To prove her words, she plucked the bucket from the ground near the tree limb where she had been sitting and strode purposefully toward the bank. Bracing her feet, she dipped the pail, bringing forth a brimming, dripping full bucket of frigid water.

Ignoring her unwanted visitor, she trekked back up the bank, passed him and headed for the house. April couldn't prevent the heavy pail from sloshing, but she wasn't about to slow her pace or use both hands and let Will Caulder see she was burdened.

"You can't keep walking away from me," he said, moving up alongside her. His long legs carried him easily. "As I've been saying, we have to discuss my claim and decide what we're going to do. I'm sure there's a friend or relative in the area who you and your sisters can stay with. Isn't there?"

She didn't break her stride. She snickered with disdain instead. "A half day has passed since you stated your *claim*, Mr. Caulder. You can't expect me to be prepared to talk about this yet, or come up with some plan to leave just to appease your wicked heart. My sisters and I aren't going anywhere. Why don't *you* go find another place to stay? Permanently."

She felt his hand on her arm, halting her. It was warm, his skin rough.

"Miss Wilde, it's in our best interests to come to a decision."

April jerked away and faced him, more shaken than she wanted to admit. "Your interest, you mean."

"I'm sorry you feel that way, but—"

"And just how else am I supposed to feel?" Her voice rose a cord. She set the pail at her feet, relieved to be free of the burden. "Do you know what it feels like to have someone barge onto your land and run you off?"

A peculiar look settled on his face. A look that was both irate and poignant. "Unfortunately, I do," he told her before his expression shifted. "Look, I know this is sudden. As I said before, I had no idea you were—" He eyed her with lingering appraisal. "All grown up. And if I could ask your father what he was thinking when he risked leaving you homeless . . . that is, in need of finding a new home . . . with caring friends or relatives. . . . A place better than this." He swept his arm around to encompass the expanse of bare land, weathered cabin and barn included. "Then I would certainly do so." He paused with an exhale of exasperation. "But, we're left with what we do know. That Justus Wilde gambled away his land to me. He did so willingly and knowingly. And I'm going to claim it."

April pressed her lips together. "I guess we'll see

about that." She picked up the heavy pail and continued on to the porch. There she halted again, ignoring the cold water that splashed. She spun about to face him with unconcealed ire. "In the meanwhile, stay away from me and my sisters, or the next shot I fire won't be a warning shot."

She slammed the door in Will's face, leaving him to watch the beams of the porch sway slightly; leaving him with the image of April Wilde's attractive backside dancing in his mind. He couldn't help but remember how she had tussled with him in the hay, then slept the night through in the hard, unforgiving chair. She had yet to brush her hair or change her clothes. She had bits of hay in the gold locks and on her brown dress with the white lace collar. And now her boots were damp from water sloshing over the pail.

Dishevelment had never looked so pretty. And, he couldn't help but think, if she looked this pretty after everything she'd been through, what would she look like freshly bathed? Smiling brightly? In a colorful dress of blue, or green to match her eyes, or pink, instead of the dreary brown?

Will backed off the porch wondering, too, what it would feel like to put a smile on her face instead of a frown. And then reality hit him; he'd probably never find out.

He turned to head back to the barn just as the front door opened again and the blond sister stepped onto the porch. He remembered her name was May, and she shyly held a platter of food in her hand. He could make out two large biscuits, a heap of potatoes and a slab of ham. In her other hand was a tin of steaming coffee.

She looked at him and chewed her bottom lip shyly. "April says not to waste a bite," she said, setting both dishes down on the old side table next to a straight-backed chair. "Leave the dishes here when you're through eating."

She then made her way down the stairs and toward the barn before he could thank her, leaving Will unsatisfied with his progress with April Wilde and staring at an offering he had no right to accept.

Chapter Three

He decided to stay out of sight after eating and having a thorough, if disturbing look around his new residence. He hoped keeping a low profile would serve to smooth April Wilde's ruffled feathers, give her time to adjust to his arrival. Besides, he hadn't expected to make the "girls" up and move out in a day. A few at best. So he could live with April's obstinence a little longer.

He made himself a lumpy bed in the barn's loft and took time to sort through his travel-weary belongings. The journey from Cripple Creek had taken him three weeks. He'd forgotten what rough terrain lay between the mining town and Colorado Springs, at the base of Pike's Peak. The changing weather and a threatening band of Cheyenne hadn't helped either. Later, he needed to wash some clothes at the river. First though, he took time to care for his horse, Tate. If not for the black he'd still be trying to make his way to the farm. The horse was as sure-footed and strong as they came.

Once he'd groomed and fed and watered Tate, Will turned his attention back to the farm. His earlier examination had left him somewhat disheartened. The cabin, he had concluded, was nothing more than a run-down shack with loose wall boards, roof tiles, and a creaking porch. He couldn't imagine what he'd find when he was able to go inside. He couldn't imagine what the Wilde sisters were doing living alone on the farm either. He wondered how long their mother had been dead, and how long they had managed to survive in the place. Didn't they know how dangerous the territory was for them, alone?

Will grumbled and forced his thoughts to shift. Repairs to the house would be necessary if his mother and sister were going to be comfortable. He also knew he couldn't demand entrance into the house to see to those repairs. Not yet. He'd caused enough injury for one day. So he decided to work in the barn instead—which had plenty of need for work itself. First he secured the wobbly animal stalls and resealed the sagging shutters. Then he replaced several missing rungs on the loft ladder. After that, Will turned his attention to the six-inch-wide hole in the roof April Wilde had made with her shotgun last night. He still couldn't believe the woman's audacity. The southern females he knew would have withered from a confrontation with him, hightailed it from the barn screaming for help—if they'd even come close to a barn. Not April. And he had to admit he admired her for standing her ground.

After last night, he'd stake everything he'd won that Miss Wilde could outmaneuver, outwit and outlast any man she wanted to. Any man who saw things differently than she did.

Except himself, of course. There was no outwitting him when it came to the deed he had in his possession. Signed and legal. With it, he intended to build a real ranchhouse, ease his mother's heartache, see a sparkle in his sister's eyes again. And give his father a bit of cheer before his ill health put him in his grave.

The end result would never replace their grand Virginia plantation. But Will was confident it would be enough to soothe most of his family's grief, give them all a future. And he, at last, would feel redemption for having failed them.

He sized up the task in front of him and with a clever scheme, scattered a cackle of chickens, much to their annoyance, as he moved his horse beneath the hole in the roof. He then pulled the repaired loft ladder over to Tate and leaned it against his strong flank.

"Easy, Tate. Whoa, boy." The black snorted but held his footing. Will began his climb up the ladder. "That's it. Steady or you and me are going to be paying the price," he urged. The black's back quivered like he understood. He remained steady until Will was high enough to reach the roof. Will began to pull down shredded pieces of wood, calculating how many boards he would need for the repair as he went. He had already figured on needing several other wood pieces for repairs to the house, and thankfully Justus Wilde's partners in cards had lost a considerable amount of gold to him the same night he'd won the deed. The money would go toward the purchase of lumber and nails among other things.

"Oh!"

Will turned his head at the sudden sound, too late realizing his action caused the ladder to shift. "Whoa,

Tate," he soothed before the horse could spook. Tate whinnied and tossed his head but stayed where he was.

"You need something, Miss Wilde?" Will said calmly.

"Oh!" he heard again, louder. Alarm tinged the feminine voice. "That's very dangerous, Mr. Caulder."

"I'm only repairing the roof," he added, seeing June Wilde's eyes widen as she took in the scene of him standing precariously on the ladder leaning against Tate's back. "And you're going to cause me to fall if you keep doing that, Miss Wilde."

His words did little good. She suddenly dropped the bucket of oats she was carrying, and cried out again as she surveyed the mess. Tate startled and blew. When he bucked, the ladder tipped, and Will was left hanging in midair.

"Great," he said sarcastically, more to himself than to the woman or the horse. And as the ladder started to lean toward the wall, the only thing Will could do was hold on. A moment later he felt a thud that rattled his insides, destroyed the ladder, and splintered the wall. Then there was nothing except air between him and the ground eight feet below.

He heard another scream, and briefly felt like shouting at June Wilde to be quiet. But then he met dirt and hay, and heard the chickens squawking again. And he couldn't breathe.

"Oh my, oh my!" June peered down at him with enormous brown eyes. "I . . . I . . . are you hurt? Of course you're hurt. I didn't mean to panic. I've just never seen anyone doing what you were doing before." She shook her hands in front of her nervously. Then she spun toward the door, pivoted back to face him again, and cried, "I'll get April. Wait here."

He had no way of going anywhere even if he

wanted to. And if Will could have talked he would have let the girl know as much in no uncertain terms.

"Don't move!" she added before her voice faded.

He rolled his eyes, wishing he could move. But his body wasn't cooperating. All he could do was grimace and try to suck air into his deflated lungs.

"There he is!" June's voice returned to grate against his senses. "He fell off the ladder."

Fell? He was sure he'd been forced off.

"Serves him right," another voice said. This one calm and collected. A voice that could only be April's. He wasn't sure which one irritated him more.

"Is he hurt?" June asked.

He peeled open his eye and saw April lean over him, a scowl on her face. "Are you hurt?" she asked matter-of-factly.

He glared at her and sucked in a huge breath, then gasped, coughed and rolled to his side.

"June, get some water," April said.

Did he detect a tinge more concern in her voice?

He continued to draw air into his lungs and inch by inch feel his body begin to sting, to pulsate, to send shooting pains through every nerve ending he never knew he had.

He groaned, the act causing more pain to slice through his already reeling head.

"Here, drink this."

He glowered at April as she placed her palm behind his head and lifted him up, pressing a cup to his lips. But he drank, sputtered, and drank again. He finally pulled away, conveying he had had enough. "I . . . I'm all right," he croaked.

He saw disappointment crease her mouth. "That's a shame," she told him, grasping him roughly under his arm. "June, help me lift him up. We'll take him to the house."

"I can walk," Will protested. "I don't need your help. I told you, I'm fine. It was just a little spill." He took another gratifying breath.

April snickered. "All I need is to have you die in our barn tonight. I can hear everyone now, talking about how we killed you so you couldn't claim our farm. No sir, Mr. Caulder. I have enough trouble in this town. I don't need more."

"Look—"

"June, grab his arm," April repeated.

June was at his side before Will could respond. She smiled weakly at him and it was all Will could do not to berate her. But much to his chagrin, he found it difficult to gain his footing, and he actually needed the two women to hold him up. His knees felt as weak and wobbly as a newborn kitten and his head as if it was screwed on backward. The only thing that appeared to have any strength at all was his heart. It had sped up considerably when April Wilde appeared. Now that she was holding him, it seemed to want to dance right out of his chest.

He fought his own sensations, knowing he had to get control, but before he could the two women had walked him to the cabin. They eased him into a rickety old wooden rocker beside the hearth. Then June backed away and April put her hands on her hips. "I suppose I should check you for broken bones," she said.

Will rubbed his throbbing head. "That's not necessary. I told you I'm fine."

"You don't think you broke anything?"

"Just bruised. The air was knocked out of me. I'm feeling better every minute."

He could tell she didn't believe him. "You just sit there for awhile. You've got a cut above your eye. Probably from the ladder splintering and flying in all directions. The *only* ladder we had," she reprimanded. "I'll get something to tend you."

He grumbled beneath his breath. She didn't need to remind him of flying debris—he had been a chunk of it. Nor scold him for breaking the ladder. Her sister had been the reason why Tate had spooked. But he let April go about her business. He could manage her cleaning a head wound. He thought. But sitting still while her hands searched him for broken bones . . . well, that just wouldn't have been possible.

Knowing so annoyed him. He was one man who enjoyed a woman's ministrations. He'd had a few brushes in the past where he'd needed some extra care. The time when he was seventeen and Abigail had a friend over for tea came to mind. He'd decided to show the ladies his horsemanship skills and ended up running into the mulberry bush. Abigail's friend had eased his scratches with liniment and his wounded ego with words of praise. Then there'd been the incident during the war when a bullet had grazed his shoulder. When one of the nurses had tended him just fine. Both incidents had been pleasurable. Made him forget about his injuries.

But April Wilde wasn't just any woman.

No, she was his adversary. She stood in the way of him completing his goal. That had to be the reason why he didn't want to accept her ministrations. He refused to believe it was because just being around her made him perspire. Made him forget his purpose and instead think about pulling her into his arms, touching her soft skin. She was prettier than a Rocky Mountain sunset and softer than the downy fur of a filly. More than that, she was intelligent, sharp-witted and keen. The main reason was because she was his rival. And he shouldn't have her tending him.

Even so, as she returned with her hands full of ointment and bandages, and a cup of something steaming, all thought of their rivalry fled from mind. He wasn't a saint. And if she wanted to tend his cut he wasn't about to stop her.

"Here," she said. "Hot broth. Drink it."

He took the cup from her hand obediently. He put the cup to his lips. It was either that, or let slip how much he enjoyed the feel of her hands on his forehead, and the smoothness of her fingers as they glided across his brow.

"Hold still," she said as he began to squirm in his chair.

He swallowed the broth.

April's hands shook as she dabbed the damp cloth on Will Caulder's brow. She was aware of his every breath, every blink of his eyes, and his surprisingly pleasant scent of fresh hay, leather, and sweat. And since she had never been so close to a man in her life, never once had to tend one, she had never felt so skittish. Just touching him was disconcerting. She felt all tingly. She had butterflies in her stomach. And yet they weren't unpleasant feelings. They were actually quite nice, which was even more disturbing.

But she couldn't *not* tend the man. She needed to make certain there wasn't any splintered wood inside his cut. If only so she could truthfully say she had done her best to help him after his fall. "Hold still," she said and placed her thumbs on either side of the two-inch gash, peering inside. She studied it closely, all too aware of his close proximity. Of his breath on her arm, and the heat from him in the air around her. If Will Caulder moved even a bit . . .

"There, it's clean now," she said and backed away. "A bit of liniment and I'll be done." She unscrewed a jar she had placed on the side table, dabbed her finger inside. "Hold this," she said and made him take the jar. Then she touched her finger to his wound. She heard his intake of breath as she did so. She told herself if he was in pain, it was his just rewards. But then she realized her action shouldn't be painful to him at all. And for some reason any suffering he was going through wasn't giving her the satisfaction she thought it should.

"Am I hurting you?" she asked him.

He glanced up at her, his brow beginning to bead with sweat. If she didn't know better, she'd think he was nervous.

"No, you're not," he answered roughly before he cleared his throat. A moment later he added, "You look like your mother."

April paused with her finger on his gash, startled by the change in subject.

"That's her picture, isn't it?" he added with a nod toward the side table.

She glanced over to the tintype. "Yes."

"You look like her, except your hair is lighter. Did you know that?"

April pursed her lips, annoyed now. "Hold still while I bandage this," she replied evasively.

"When did she die?" Will pressed. He was bobbing his knee up and down at a fast pace, and his free hand was pressed to it like he was holding on for dear life.

April grabbed the jar from his other hand. "My mother died a long time ago, Mr. Caulder. Didn't my *father* tell you that much? Or didn't he know? We sent him word, but since he never came home for her burial we never knew if he had received it." She gathered the linen swatch from the table and began to wrap it around Will's head. "Of course knowing Justus Wilde, he wouldn't have come home anyway. He had a gold claim to dig, riches to find. Now," she added. "I'll thank you not to ask any more personal questions about my family. We're none of your business."

Will halted her hand in midair as she circled his head. She darted her gaze to his, only to find his blue eyes had turned to a smoldering shade of purple.

"I didn't mean to rile you, Miss Wilde," he told her. "You're right of course, it was a personal question to ask. I'll try not to make the same mistake again. I was merely interested in knowing how long you three sisters have been alone."

Shaken, April twisted away from his hold, tied off his bandage and stepped away from him. She took a steadying breath. "Your interest isn't appreciated, Mr. Caulder," she told him just as the front door opened.

April turned to see May precede Daniel Moss into the house. Her tension rose as she stared at the sheriff. He was either going to help or harm them. She wished she knew which one. Moss was one of the few people she knew who had remained cordial to her over the years, but he'd never been overly friendly. He would tip his hat to her, acknowledge her, but there was always a wariness about him. One that made her watch her step.

She wasn't sure what to expect now, but she'd had no choice but to send for him. She walked his way, acknowledging him with a nod of her head. "Sheriff."

"What's this all about, Miss Wilde?" Moss asked her. "Your sister told me something about an intruder."

Behind her, Will rose from the rocker. The sheriff gave him a once-over, noting the bandage.

"This man is claiming my father gambled away our home to him," she said before Will could speak. "We came home last night to find him in the barn. He hurt himself while trying to make repairs out there. Repairs he has no business making."

"I have proof," Will stated. "Proof of ownership."

April pivoted, her gaze intent. "A piece of paper is not proof enough."

"A signed, legal document is," Will countered.

"You've got this document handy, Mister . . . Mister?"

"Caulder, Sheriff. Will Caulder." He reached into his shirt pocket and extracted the deed.

Moss took it and began to scan it. "How'd you come by this?" he asked.

"I was in a card game, draw. Justus Wilde, Pedro Rodriguez, Lyonel Sims, and me." He glanced at April and her sisters, before facing the sheriff again. "The date was September twentieth. A Saturday night after the miners had shut down for the day."

Not even two months ago.

"Go on," the sheriff prodded.

"Wilde and Sims had made a decent strike that day. They had already taken their gold to the assayer and were flaunting some hard coin. Wilde was drunk, there was no doubt about that. And he was cocky. He kept saying that he couldn't lose that day, due to the earlier strike.

"Sims dealt a hand that we both thought we could win. But by then Sims had lost a considerable amount to me. I kept upping Wilde's bet until he decided to wager the deed to this place.

"I tried to get him to reconsider. But—" He halted

briefly and shrugged. "He thought his three queens had him the hand. They didn't. I had four tens."

April's eyes burned. Her ears drummed. This was how her whole life had been turned upside down? "He was drunk. You said so yourself. You took advantage of him, Mr. Caulder."

"Did he think you had cheated him when he'd sobered up?" Sheriff Moss asked Will.

Will shook his head. "He never sobered. I heard from Sims that he died that night."

April's jaw dropped. She heard May and June sobbing. "You expect us to believe all this?" she asked, incredulous. "How convenient, Mr. Caulder. You just happened to be at the right place at the right time? You win the deed to our land and our father dies before anyone can question the legitimacy of the claim?

"Get out of this house," she ground out. "I don't care if you have a dozen broken bones from your fall. Get out of this house. Get off this land."

"Miss Wilde," Sheriff Moss interceded. He held out his hand to quiet her. "I wouldn't be too rash if I were you. Your Pa may have been drunk, but the deed Mr. Caulder has looks real enough. And if his story holds up, his claim might be legal."

April felt as if an icy winter wind had just blown over her skin. "Surely—"

"Now, I'm not saying it's definitely legal," he added quickly. "I'm just saying we need to investigate a bit to see if Mr. Caulder could have a legit claim."

"How do we know? What do we do?" April folded her arms. She was suddenly so cold she could feel herself shaking. And yet she wasn't about to show either man how afraid she was.

"I think the circuit judge needs to decide this dilemma," the sheriff told her. He was a big man. His dark hair was graying. April had always hoped, if necessary, the sheriff would prove himself fair. His words canceled that hope. Moss knew as well as anyone that the circuit judge, Judge Percy Claymore, was Sadie Claymore's husband and Cirrus Claymore's father.

Sadie had done a good job turning the townsfolk of Ruley against April. She'd told anyone who would listen about how April had rebuffed Sadie's attempts to help after Sarah Wilde's death. But what Sadie failed to tell them was what Cirrus Claymore, then seventeen, had wanted in return for the food his mother sent to the girls. At first April tried to tell herself she was mistaken about Cirrus and the innuendos he made when he brought her a basket. But when he tried to kiss her one afternoon, she'd realized how right she'd been. She'd slapped him hard and told him never to return. When he'd relayed his version of the story to Sadie, she must have not been too pleased. April didn't know what Cirrus said, what version of the truth he told, but April had been paying the price for his words and his mother's anger for seven long years.

And now, if Judge Claymore was put in charge of deciding who owned Justus Wilde's homestead, April knew she might as well start packing.

"Mr. Caulder," the sheriff said. "This dilemma isn't going to be decided any time soon. And I imagine you're not real wanted around here. But since I can't make you leave, either, I suggest you stay in the barn and out of the Wilde sisters' way for the time being. I can't stop you from making repairs to the place either, but that's a risk you'll be taking if this thing is resolved in the girls' favor. Up to you.

"Miss April," he added then, facing her, "You go on into town and get yourself a lawyer."

"A lawyer?"

"You'd be smart to have someone represent you," Moss answered.

Shocked, April could only nod.

"Let's go, Caulder," he added. The sheriff returned his hat to his head, tipping it, like he always did, in farewell, before he escorted Will from the house.

April continued to stand in the middle of the room, frozen in place.

"What are we going to do?" May asked after a few moments.

Beside her, June bawled loudly.

Over the years April had heard those same words often from her sisters. The day of their mother's death had been the first. She hadn't known then and she didn't know now. She only knew she was weary of hearing those words. Weary of having the responsibility of comforting her sisters when she needed comfort herself. But she knew she had to be strong for them. That she couldn't let them see her fear. And she couldn't let them down. She'd be letting her mother down if she did. And she'd never allow that to happen.

She'd have to digest Moss's words, decide if a lawyer was a possibility or not, or come up with another plan. In the meanwhile, she forced a smile. "Everything will be fine," she assured May and June. "No one is going to take our home away from us." She only wished she believed her words.

Chapter Four

April drove the wagon away from the house in silence the following morning, her sisters beside her. Her mind too unsettled after Sheriff Moss and Will Caulder vacated her house, she'd sat up most of the night thinking and praying. So far, she had no answer on how to get Will Caulder off her land. Which didn't please her. And which didn't leave her much to go on since she needed to make a decision. Sheriff Moss had suggested she hire an attorney. Cirrus Claymore was the only attorney in Ruley. She still shuddered in revulsion whenever she saw him. Only weeks ago he'd once again told her that he'd still consider her for a wife. Now more mature than when she'd been twelve, she'd politely told him she wasn't interested. But if she had to rely on him to represent her—before his father—what would he think? Especially since she had little money to pay him.

Which made her other idea—attempting to pay Will Caulder off—just as impractical. Unless perhaps Edwin Talbot's bank would loan her the money. She could work to pay the debt back.

Her idea list stopped at two. Three if she wanted to reconsider her first idea—Caulder's demise. But of course she'd never do that.

She glanced back at the house in the distance behind them, and wondered if she shouldn't return. *He* was there alone now and April didn't trust him in the least. But if ever there was a morning she needed to be in church it was this Sunday morning, feeling more than a mite weary, more than a mite angry. Much more than a mite, actually. And all, she decided, because she'd finally given in to the temptation to dream about her future, Friday night after the dance just before she'd discovered Will Caulder in her barn.

She should have known better.

With a forlorn sigh, April pulled her gaze away from the farm and decided Caulder couldn't do much harm while she and May and June were gone. And surely, since God hadn't spoken directly to her about the situation, He'd give Pastor Johnson a very detailed message for her. Then she'd know what course to take.

She could already hear the Sabbath bell ringing, a reminder that today was worship day. Time to forget her own troubles and focus on church. The road leading to the house of worship was already lined with other rigs. Children scampered around the grass and men and women stood talking in small groups.

As always, when the Wilde sisters appeared, people paused to watch. April was used to their curiosity, but this morning their regard seemed a bit more than usual. Had Sheriff Moss talked about Will Caulder's arrival? Or were they just more interested now that the three girls had gone to the Harvest Social?

"Miss June," said a young man as they passed by. He slipped off his hat and bowed slightly. "It sure was enjoyable dancing with you Friday night."

June giggled and April smiled for the first time since the dance. Then she caught sight of Edwin Talbot motioning her toward him where he'd staked out a place for her to park the buckboard.

"Good day to you Miss April, Miss June, May," the immaculately dressed bank manager greeted them as he caught the harness and pulled the horses to a stop. He moved to the side of the rig and helped May down, then June.

"Good day," April replied as she stepped down from the rig on her own.

"What's going on at your place?" Edwin asked then, his attention on May. "I heard there's a strange man there. It's really not wise, May, to allow him to stay. You know how difficult it's already been for me to court you, what with the way everyone feels about your family. Now this could lead to my customers . . ."

April quickly turned away as May and June began to explain. She didn't think she could stand Edwin's whining or listen to May's explanation just now.

Sheriff Moss, it was evident, hadn't had the same problem.

She headed into the whitewashed church, the newest building in Ruley, complete with steeple and bell and real pews. She stood in a pew toward the back, ignoring animated whispers and stares all around her. No one spoke to her as they shuffled about for other seats. No one sat next to her either, which left plenty of room for May, Edwin, and June when they at last joined her.

Pastor Johnson began to lead them in a soulful version of *Oh Glorious Savior*, one of April's favorite hymns. Then they all sat down and he greeted them.

"I hope we've caught up on our rest since Friday night's social."

April wished she could have answered yes. Instead his words made her eyes droop as she realized how little sleep she'd had since then. She blinked rapidly and tried to focus on his words.

"Today we continue our study in the Book of Exodus," he went on. "Open your Bibles to the twelfth chapter please."

An hour later April was as confused as ever. Nothing in the message had spoken to her heart. The story of the Israelites being set free after years of captivity wasn't exactly something she could relate to. She didn't feel like she was a prisoner. She wanted to be exactly where she was—and not have to leave.

Fine, she thought, exiting the pews with the others. Since she wasn't getting an answer just when she needed it most, she'd just have to figure her own way out of the mess her miserable father had placed her in.

"Miss Wilde," she heard then as she exited the church.

April glanced up to see Cirrus Claymore waiting for her. He patted his black hair and pushed back his shoulders as she stifled a groan and coolly nodded.

"I heard about your terrible predicament," he said, maneuvering himself in front of her. She could smell his stifling cologne and felt her nose twitch as she sidestepped him, only to have him move alongside her. He was twenty and seven now. He was tall and lanky and like the seventeen-year-old who had pressed wet lips to hers years before, still bumbling.

"Predicament?" she replied, feigning ignorance. She continued to walk. "I'm not sure I know what you mean, Mr. Claymore. Perhaps you have me confused with someone else. But thank you for your concern."

"No he doesn't," June protested from behind her. "I told him everything, April. He asked me about Mr. Caulder and I told him. He said he could help."

April groaned again. She should have confided to June as she had to May what Cirrus Claymore had done a long time ago. Had she only done so she could have avoided June's interference now.

"Your sister is right. She told me all about the man trying to take your land. And you know, as well as I do, that I'm the only one who can assist you in your quest to retain it, Miss Wilde," Cirrus said.

She was sure he thought so. But April wasn't yet ready to concede.

"I'm confident that with me by your side everything will work out fine. We will make a great team."

April managed a tight smile. "That's kind of you, Mr. Claymore, but I believe I already have a solution." She swallowed the lie.

"You do?" His smile failed.

"You do?" repeated June excitedly.

Cirrus's expression hardened. "Perhaps you could share your solution then," he added. He lifted a thin brow, suspicion there. "From what Sheriff Moss says, you have no other solution than to obtain an attorney. Me, since there are no others. Unless you've decided not to fight for your land. Is that your solution? Then perhaps you're ready to move on? Perhaps to marriage?"

April clutched her Bible tighter, bile burning in her throat. He either saw right through her, or was confident no matter what the outcome, he'd be on the winning side. And he knew as well as she did that she needed him if she were going to get his father on her side.

The thought made her stomach sour. She seemed to never be able to get away from this man. Only a week ago, on her way to the mercantile, she'd found Cirrus roughing up the Elliotts' oldest son, Tim. She'd heard the boy cry out ahead on the road, and saw Cirrus holding the fourteen-year-old by the ear and forcing him to pick up a crate of spilled apples.

Cirrus had been taking the fruit home to his mother when Tim had dashed across the road in front of his buggy on his way to get Doc Edwards for his ailing mother. The crate had spilled when the horse spooked. Instead of understanding Tim's haste, Cirrus had chased Tim down and brought him back to pick up the mess.

April had picked up the apples herself and prodded Tim to be on his way. And Cirrus had smugly told her that if she and he were to ever have children together, their son would be much better behaved.

Was she destined to marry this man? He'd proven himself to be as persistent as a squirrel collecting winter food. Her opinion of him ranked dead even with her opinion of Will Caulder. Contempt was hard to shadow. But what other alternative did she have than to accept his help? "I can't compensate you, Mr. Claymore," she said.

He smiled with what could only be satisfaction and April noted his dark, almost black eyes, straight black hair that fell over his ears, and his thin eyebrows and long chin. He wasn't unattractive on the outside, but the core of him, the invisible part, she found completely unappealing. "I'm sure we could think of some sort of payment, Miss Wilde," he drawled. "I'll be glad to accept something other than money for my services."

That's what bothered her so much. "I'll consider your offer, Mr. Claymore," she said, "while deciding what I can offer you in return. If I agree to accept your services I could come to your office tomorrow afternoon to discuss the situation."

"That'll be fine, Miss Wilde," he beamed. "I'll look forward to the visit."

April tried to smile back, but couldn't quite force herself to do so.

Will heard the wagon approaching before he saw it, the sound of the harness slowly escalating. He stopped hammering the nail in the roof and turned toward the sound, even while telling himself not to. The sisters were returning. *She* was returning. In spite of himself he felt a twinge of anticipation and immediately fought the feeling aside. He had a job to do, a goal to meet. One that didn't include worrying about April Wilde.

Still, as much as he told himself not to, he watched the wagon roll into the yard and the three sisters jump from the wooden seat. All three stared at him high on the house's rooftop, disapproval stamped on each attractive face.

April was the first to pull her attention away. Without a word she entered the house. When the other two fell into step behind her, Will forced his attention back to work securing loose roof boards. Their silence was welcome, he told himself. It meant April Wilde was still pondering her next step. That no one in town had given her any better advice than the sheriff had.

For some reason she'd not been overly pleased with Moss's recommendation that she acquire an attorney and have a judge rule on his claim. She'd paled visibly when Moss had made his suggestion. Will had needed to bite his tongue to keep from asking her why. He'd never been in a position quite like this before. Remembering that she was his rival instead of someone he could offer assistance. The role was new to him. His whole life had been spent solving problems; first as the estate manager for his family's vast holdings, then as a Lieutenant in the War. Since then his sole purpose had been to regain stability for his family. Working out trouble was natural to him.

Except this time. He couldn't offer April Wilde any assistance. He'd be throwing away the very thing he'd strived so long to obtain if he did.

Will banged the hammer hard against the rooftop before noticing May Wilde standing beneath the eaves, staring up at him. In her hand was a plate brimming with appetizing food. His mouth watered, his stomach grumbled. And he'd never felt so disgusted with himself in his life.

"April says—"

"—not to waste it," he finished for the girl.

May nodded, her gentle blue eyes filled with compassion. She headed back to the porch and Will heard her slide the platter onto the table before she retreated into the house.

April noticed him an hour later as he sat on the front steps, his shirt taut against his muscled back. Her breath hitched a little and her stomach quivered as she watched his muscles flex. She set the kettle she was carrying on the stove's hot plate and forgot about everything else except watching him. He stood up, placed his plate on the table, then walked over to the water bucket where he drew a dipper of water and brought it to his lips.

April swallowed tightly. Never in her life had she

been so fascinated by a man. Just the sight of him made her feel things she'd never felt before. Made her question things she'd never questioned before. Like what it would be like to have a man around all the time, repairing things, like the roof, and eating her food. She looked at his plate again, empty now, and a sense of satisfaction settled over her. Had he enjoyed his meal? Would he want more if it were offered to him?

Her gaze still following him, she watched him stretch his arms over his head. His flannel tightened even more, leaving no doubt that he was firmly corded beneath his clothes. And then he reached into his shirt front pocket and pulled out a piece of paper, and April snapped out of her musings.

The deed. The deed to her land, her future. How could she think of Will Caulder with anything but disdain?

"April?"

"What?" she barked, then wished she hadn't. She turned her back to the window, determined not to give her enemy another thought. "I'm sorry, May. Did you need me?"

"I understand," May replied. Her gaze darted beyond April. "He is handsome, isn't he?"

April sniffed and began to untie her apron. "I hadn't noticed," she lied. "As far as I'm concerned he's the most repulsive-looking man on earth. On the outside as well as the inside."

May smiled slightly and April knew she hadn't fooled her sister. "But it doesn't really matter, does it? He'll be gone in a few days. I hope we never see him again."

"The mountains have disappeared," May went on.

"It looks like snow's headed this way. Are you going to make him sleep in the barn again?"

"I'm not making him do anything," April countered. "He's chosen his path." Before May could reply—or censor April like April thought she was going to do, she added, "I'm going to collect his plate. Watch the kettle, would you?"

She quickly grabbed her coat and stepped outside. It was also time to collect Mr. Caulder's deed for her inevitable meeting with Cirrus tomorrow.

Will paused with the ladle near his mouth when he saw April on the porch. She was buttoning her coat, a bulky, overstuffed wool covering of nondescript brown that reached her ankles and hid her curves. Unlike the dress she'd been wearing yesterday when he'd sat in her rocker while she tended his head. Then he'd gotten a close-up look at her narrow waist, her smooth skin. And her fresh scent, like the fragrance of warm summer flowers, had nearly knocked him out of the chair.

Now, as then, though, her eyes were tired, her brow was knit and her lips pressed tightly together. All due to his claim. Will tossed the ladle back in the bucket and waited for her to approach him. "Miss Wilde," he acknowledged when her stride deposited her in front of him.

"Mr. Caulder." She inched her chin up. "I need to take your deed to town with me tomorrow."

"So you've decided to listen to the sheriff and retain an attorney?" The wind was beginning to pick up. Will noted April lifted her coat collar over her neck, and her hair, the brilliant color of fall wheat, began to dance about her face.

"What I'm planning to do is none of your business, Mr. Caulder. I just need the deed."

Will smiled indulgently. "It's my deed, Miss Wilde. You don't think I'd just turn it over to you, surely? Without knowing what your plans are? You could tear it up. Burn it. Any number of things. Good try, darling, but—"

"Don't you dare call me darling, you . . . you . . ." April forced her mouth closed, fisted her hands at her sides. "Mr. Caulder," she began again, more in control. "You are the cheat here, not me. You've forced me to solicit advice from a professional. And *he* will need to see the deed."

Will felt the conviction of her truth. He was the one who had taken advantage of her father. And April could have stolen the deed the night she'd knocked him witless. Still. "I came by this property when your father chose to gamble it away," he said to defend himself. "I didn't force him."

April just snickered derisively. "Who are you trying to convince, Mr. Caulder, you or me?"

Will shifted uncomfortably. "The deed stays with me at all times. If you want an attorney to look it over I go with you."

"Go with me?" She brushed her blowing hair from her face with a dainty hand and blinked, as if considering his words. She seemed to latch onto the idea. "Very well, if you insist. We'll leave after my chores are done."

"I'll help you then—with the chores. What would you like me to do?"

She turned on her heels and began to walk away. "Your kind of help is not welcome here," she tossed over her shoulder.

They headed for Ruley the following mid-morning. An inch of snow covered the ground, turning the brown landscape into a brilliant white, but the sky was already as big and blue as any day after an autumn storm had swept through.

April sat atop the buckboard, taking pleasure in the feel of the warming sun on her face and the snow-peaked mountains in the distance, despite the hard lump in her stomach. For the life of her she wished she could forget Will Caulder was her traveling companion, behind her on his horse.

Earlier, when she'd entered the barn to milk the cows and feed the chickens, she'd watched him roll out of his pallet in the loft. He'd grumbled, burrowed into one of the blankets she'd had May give him, and with an armload of clothes, silently disappeared outside. He'd returned when she was harnessing Samson for the ride into town, dressed in his dungarees, boots and another flannel, but with the rest of his pile of clothes dripping water. His hair was damp as well, and he was shivering. He stopped to watch April scrape mud from her boots and hay from her dress and she pretended not to notice the self-satisfied grin that lit up his face, the one that told her she wouldn't have needed to scrape anything from her shoes if she'd accepted his offer to help with the chores.

Grumbling herself, she'd marched to the house to indulge herself in a rare warm bath, her ire smoothed when she thought of Will suffering through his own bath in the frigid Platte.

She took her time dressing, too, borrowing May's pale yellow skirt to go with her own white bodice and cornflower-blue jacket, and shining her boots until they sparkled.

Feeling presentable again, she'd finally decided she'd put off going to Cirrus's office as long as she could. She'd made her way outside to round up her deed-carrying tag-along, only to find him sitting on the steps, eating the hot steaming oats and biscuits May had taken him. The black flannel he wore, with his still-damp hair curling at the edges, made her insides begin to stir—again.

She'd stomped past him, annoyed—again—with herself. When was her system going to stop such nonsense? The man was her enemy. And why had she told May to feed him? He would have been long gone, searching for meals, if she'd not been so compassionate.

"I'm leaving now. If you have something better to do with your time, I'll take the deed and go myself," she'd said tersely, and decided not to wait for his response. She'd climbed onto the wagon seat instead.

Now halfway to town, with the sun high and Ruley still more than a mile away, she was all too aware of the quiet, the isolation, and Mr. Caulder's close proximity. The nearest farmhouse was the Elliotts'. She could barely see the smoke spiraling from their chimney.

She'd never been alone with a man. She felt awkward and jittery. She should have been afraid. Caulder could easily harm her and no one would know. But for some reason fear wasn't mingled with her anxiety and self-consciousness.

She glanced behind her, deciding to keep a better eye on him even so, but he didn't seem to be paying her any mind. His hat was low over his brow and his gaze fixed on the landscape. He was obviously not concerned about her. Or wrapped up in thoughts of her. She was just a small bit of dust on his shoulder. One he was about to fling off and forget about.

He, on the other hand, represented the biggest threat she'd ever encountered. Worse than sheer survival.

The one hour, one day at a time kind of survival, she was used to. Even at the young age of twelve she'd known just what to do so she and her sisters would survive their mother's death. So they could stay together. She knew how to use a gun, build a fire . . . and ignore the pain in her heart.

But Caulder was smart. Cunning. April had to outwit him if she was going to keep her home. She'd have to think like him.

With little experience in such things the task seemed daunting. So, she'd begin by hoping Cirrus could sway his father to rule in her favor. And hope not to end up worse off for doing so.

To that end, she was grateful Will Caulder was going to be with her during her visit to the attorney. When he'd proposed going with her yesterday, she'd seen a way to use his presence to her advantage. She was certain Cirrus was going to press his attentions on her again in exchange for his services. And with Will along, that'd be one less problem she'd face.

The attorney greeted her in the stylish foyer of the law firm his father had established prior to taking the bench before April could be announced by his law clerk.

Will noted Cirrus Claymore was tall, with dark hair and a pasty complexion. He also had a smug smile on his oblong face as he approached April. As if he shared a special secret with her. One he was pleased about.

"April," he said with familiarity, his arms extended. "I'm glad you've finally seen the light. You've made me a very happy man. I'm sure this will be the beginning of a wonderful liaison."

April rose from the sofa, her chin more prominently set than Will had ever seen it, which was considerable since he was the prime source of her current irritation. "Mr. Claymore," she replied firmly, as Claymore took her hand and tried to bring it to his lips. "I'll thank you not to call me by my given name." She failed to return his smile. She tugged her hand from his. "I am your client. Nothing more. And the liaison you refer to will be strictly professional."

"Now April," the attorney countered, his cheeks shading. "Don't go spoiling this before we've even begun. We have an agreement." His smile remained, but it now seemed off-kilter. He had dropped his hands to his sides when April drew away from him. Now Will noticed him flexing them. "You know I've looked forward to this day for a long time. It's just taken you longer to realize what we both know."

"I don't know any such thing," April was quick to say. Will could feel her mounting anxiety. Her body was shaking and her voice quivered. "And we have no agreement. We've yet to determine what the agreement will be. But I can assure you it will be strictly professional."

Will chose to rise from his seat at that moment. The attorney hadn't noticed him next to April. But Will was more than intrigued by this little display. Any man worth his salt could tell Claymore was making it clear April owed him more than money for his services. A common ploy used by men who sought the affections of an attractive woman. She was just as clearly letting him know she was not going to reciprocate—something not so common.

Despite his and April's own contention, he wasn't about to stand aside and let the attorney assume things April had not agreed to. And since he didn't like Claymore on sight, especially the way he was staring at April, the task was easy.

The lawyer became aware of Will as soon as he gained his feet. Will practically brushed April's shoulder with his own.

Claymore's deportment shifted. "I'm sorry, do you have an appointment? I don't believe I was informed—"

"I'm with Miss Wilde," Will replied casually. He planted his feet and removed his hat, enjoying the man's discomfiture.

"Mr. Caulder is the man claiming to own my land," April added. "I brought him along because, well, he doesn't trust me. He insisted on bringing the deed himself."

Will questioned her explanation. He was beginning to think she had set him up to join her simply so she wouldn't have to be alone with Claymore. Which, after meeting the man, he could understand.

Claymore stared at Will with what appeared to be distaste, sizing him up. But when Will stared right back, the bravado Will had first sensed in the man when he assumed April was by herself seemed to dissipate. His smugness dimmed. "Well, since we're all here then, I suppose we can do nothing else but retire to my office for further discussion. *Miss Wilde*," he prompted with a frown and extended his hand toward the office door. "Mr. Caulder."

Without thought, Will placed his hand on the small of April's back and followed her into the large, richly appointed office. Once inside he motioned to a shiny leather chair for her to take. Claymore circled his desk and dropped into a similar one behind it while Will remained standing, his gaze scanning the shelves of books and bric-a-brac scattered around the office.

"Aren't you going to sit down?" April whispered to him.

"I don't plan on staying long," he told her.

When she bit her bottom lip, clearly anxious, it furthered his assessment. She really didn't want to be alone with Claymore.

"Perhaps we could begin with an explanation, Mr. Caulder." Claymore took pen in hand as he spoke. "Why do you think Miss Wilde's property is now yours?"

Will merely smiled at the man's poor attempt to find out information Will had no intention of providing. "I don't think that's why we're here." He turned his hat in his hand slowly. "I came as a favor to Miss Wilde. I'll show you my deed. You can make of it what you want and advise her accordingly. After all, you're Miss Wilde's counsel, not mine."

Claymore turned another shade of red and began to shuffle paperwork on his desk. "Yes, well, I was merely hoping we could settle this dispute here and now instead of in court. In order to spare Miss Wilde any further heartache."

Will finally gave the man a bit of regard. He didn't believe Claymore, but he couldn't fault him for trying. Perhaps he wasn't as inept as Will thought. "Unfortunately, that's not going to happen. Unless Miss Wilde comes to realize she can't win."

"Unless I come to realize?" April queried. "You're the one, Mr. Caulder, who needs to realize people can't just walk onto someone's property and claim it for their own."

"Now, now, April. Let's not be churlish," Claymore scolded.

"Churlish?" April rose from the chair. "I'm not a child, Mr. Claymore. Nor do I choose to be treated like one. If saving my home means expressing my anger, and telling the truth, then so be it. And if you don't care for my attitude, then perhaps we won't be able to come to an agreement after all." She stepped away from her chair, her intention to find the door.

"No! Wait!" called Cirrus. He leaped from his chair to grab April's arm. "I . . . you needn't become so upset. You have good reason to talk to Mr. Caulder in such a way. Please sit down, Miss Wilde, and we'll continue. Now then, may I see the deed please?"

As April sat on the edge of the chair, Will took the deed from his shirt pocket and smoothed the folds, then tossed it on Claymore's desk. The attorney began to study it. At length, he set the document aside and glanced to April and Will.

"My father was not in his right mind when he signed the deed," April said. "Mr. Caulder has admitted as much. My father was drunk. He died that same night."

"You've had this document in your possession since the date it was signed, Mr. Caulder?"

Will snatched the deed from Claymore's desk without answering. "You've seen my proof with your own eyes. As I stated before, we aren't here to question me. Advise your client what's best for her." With that he tipped his head and turned on his heel.

"Where are you going?" April rose abruptly from her chair again, worry in her tone.

Will pivoted and saw the same worry reflected in her smoldering green eyes. "Nowhere. I was just going to wait by the door." He wasn't, of course, but her reaction changed his mind.

"Actually, you should leave now, Mr. Caulder," Cirrus broke in. "So I can attend my . . . ah, client, in private."

"That won't be necessary," she tossed back.

"But . . ." Claymore protested. "Anything you and I discuss needs to be confidential."

"You've seen the deed." April slowly sank back down on the edge of the chair, her hands clasped around the strings of her reticule. Despite her anxiousness, Will couldn't help but compare her to a bright spring day after a gentle rain. She was fresh and fragrant. Her yellow and blue outfit, unlike the normal drab browns she wore, enhanced the color of her hair and eyes, and flattered her gentle curves.

Will had nearly forgotten all about finishing his delicious breakfast when she'd stepped onto the porch before their trip, so mesmerized was he by her. And riding behind her on the journey hadn't helped. Her gentle fragrance had continued to waft by, and her golden hair, shimmering in the sun, kept escaping her bonnet. She'd been fidgety, clenching and unclenching the reins with her gloved hands as she led the horse. And from time to time he'd watched her massage her neck, stirring in him the fondest desire to climb aboard the wagon and rub the area for her.

All the while her stature had remained stiff and her lovely face fraught with concern. As it was now. If he didn't know better, Will would think she despised Claymore more than she did him.

"You just need to tell me if the deed is legitimate," she went on to the pasty-faced attorney. "And if so, what our next step is. Does Judge Claymore—your father—need to rule on who stays and who leaves?"

Claymore pressed his lips together, eyed Will, then addressed April. "The deed appears to be legal. There are two witnesses' signatures. And yes, our next step is to hold a hearing before Judge Claymore and present our case for denial based on the fact that your father was inebriated."

"Very well. Now as to our agreement, I believe I have an idea that will suit." She continued to twist the strings of her reticule. "I . . . you remember I told you I could not compensate you with money."

"This is not the time—"

"But it is." She rose from the chair. She took a steadying breath and notched her chin high. "I can compensate you by cleaning your office for a period of time. Or—"

"That's absurd," Claymore exclaimed.

Will had to agree with the attorney.

"Very well. I'll mend your clothing then. Or prepare you some meals."

"April. I won't discuss—"

"Miss Wilde," she insisted.

Claymore heaved a sigh of exasperation and darted his angry gaze to Will. "You understand this is why I feel the need to take charge of her, don't you? Her insolence is enough to drive a man mad."

Will watched April's mouth drop open. "How dare you talk about me as if I weren't in the room."

"Well, it's no more than you deserve." Cirrus planted his palms on his desk. "Now stop all this nonsense of mending and cleaning. I find the very thought distasteful."

"I have nothing else to offer," April informed him. "Nothing."

"Except your company." The room grew quiet. "Which is what I ask for. Lawrence Tuttle and Violet Snowden are getting married next week. Surely you can accompany me."

April gnawed her bottom lip. "I . . . I would not be welcome at such an event, Mr. Claymore. Nor do I wish to attend a wedding when I'm not friends with the guests of honor. I suppose if you won't accept labor in return for your law services I will have to look elsewhere for advice."

Will couldn't believe what he was hearing. She was going to throw away her representation, risk her farm, just so she wouldn't have to go to a wedding with Claymore? But no, it was more than that. Even he knew if she went one place with Claymore he would demand another. And it was obvious she truly despised the man. Why?

Claymore rose to his full height and cleared his throat. His gaze hardened. "Very well, Miss Wilde. Perhaps I am pushing you a bit. Perhaps you need more time to come to realize that I want only what's best for you. I have waited this long. I can wait longer. I accept your offer of labor. You may tidy this office once a week for the next month in exchange for my time in presenting your case before Judge Claymore."

April sighed visibly. "Very well. We do have an agreement then. Don't we, Mr. Caulder?" She turned Will's way, expecting him to answer. "Don't we?"

"Yes. It appears so."

"I will expect to hear from you when Judge Claymore sets a hearing date, Mr. Claymore." She hurried toward the exit. "Good day."

Once outside the law firm again, she paused, took a deep breath, then hurried over to the buckboard. Will halted alongside her, watched her grasp Solomon's bridle and press her face into the horse's nose. Her shoulders quivered.

"You want to explain what that was all about?" he asked her.

She didn't bother to turn around. Her weight sagged and she sniffed. "Just remember what he agreed to," she replied.

"Meaning you think he'll demand something more?

Something you're not willing to give? Meaning he'll try to change the agreement if he can? So you needed a witness along just to be safe and you used me for that end?"

She glanced his way and blinked slowly. "Yes."

Chapter Five

April was still as tightly wound as a henhouse with a wolf at the door when she was more than halfway home. Indeed, she felt as if a wolf was at *her* door. Two of them. She wondered now if Cirrus would properly represent her before his father. Surely, this time, he had heard her loud and clear. She wasn't interested in him and her affections were not for sale.

She had used Will's presence for impact. And she didn't care that he was none too pleased about it. Both men were trying to use her for their ill-gotten gains. What was the difference?

Hopefully Cirrus understood now, and would give up pursuing her while still providing her adequate counsel. He didn't know—and didn't need to know— that she loathed Will as much as she did Cirrus. And it felt mighty good to have outwitted them both. Mighty good. Even if she wasn't foolish enough to think she'd won much more than a reprieve. Her effort had left her exhausted. Already her relief was spinning back toward fear.

She ignored the small quiet voice inside her head that told her not to be afraid and clicked the reins over Solomon's back.

"It'll be dark soon."

April jumped in the seat and turned to see Will on horseback beside her. She hadn't expected him to catch up to her. He'd stayed in town once they'd left Cirrus's office.

"That was uncalled for," she ground out.

"What was?" he asked nonchalantly.

"You know what. Sneaking up on me like you did."

"Don't tell me you didn't see me. I've been riding alongside you for several minutes now." He had a too-even look on his face. Was he deliberately trying to irritate her? If so, it was working, but she wasn't going to let him know it.

"I'm not in the habit of glancing around to see if I'm being followed, Mr. Caulder. I suppose I should be more careful. It's obviously not safe any longer to travel to and from town."

He looked at her with mischief reflected in his sky-blue eyes. "Good idea. You should pay more attention to your surroundings, Miss Wilde."

April fumed inside. "I didn't ask for your advice," she tossed back. "You're nothing but an easterner who doesn't know a thing about the west. Like how to be honorable and upright. Instead you prey on the weak. Why don't you just go back east and leave us all alone?"

She saw him immediately grip the reins of his horse tighter, his easy manner disappearing. His sharp re-action to her words surprised her. She hadn't expected

them to bother him. But something she'd said truly
disturbed him.

Was it the part about being honorable and upright
or preying on the weak? Or was it her reference to
going back east? He'd told June that he'd fought in
the just-ended war. He'd obviously lost with the rest
of the southern Rebels. Most likely whatever he
owned if he needed her land so desperately. Which
wasn't her problem at all. He deserved her caustic
words and more. He'd earned her wrath, not her sym-
pathies. And so she fought the latter away.

"Now that's a fine recommendation, Miss Wilde."
He quickly regained his composure. It was as if she
hadn't scolded him at all. "I'd do just what you proposed; kiss the west good-bye, and return to the beautiful valleys of Virginia. If, that is, I had a home to go
home to."

It was April's turn to frown. "It's not my fault you
chose the losing side," she hurled. "Nor that you lost
everything."

He turned his gaze her way. "How do you know I
chose the losing side? Or that I lost everything?"

"Well, you said you were from Virginia. Virginians
sided with the southern cause. And it's clear you don't
have much."

He failed to reply, obviously contemplating her
words. "We had a plantation, true," he finally said,
"but our workers were free. Always had been. My
grandfather didn't believe in slavery."

"Then you fought for the North?"

He shrugged.

She shook her head, confused. But she wasn't about
to probe him further. His past was none of her concern. "It doesn't matter. Someone stole your property,
you're stealing mine."

"Theft doesn't come with a deed of ownership," he stated.

"It does in this case," she rebutted and concentrated on Solomon's reins.

He was silent as he kept pace with her, his horse clopping easily alongside her wagon. She hoped he was rethinking his claim. Maybe if she kept trying to get through to him that what he was doing was wrong, it would work. Before Judge Claymore gave him her home.

"I wanted you to know," he said when they'd gone another distance. "The house is in pretty bad shape, and it's small. It would cost just as much to repair it as replace it. Or enlarge it. Since my family will be arriving sooner than later, I ordered some supplies while I was in town. Mr. Dortch is having them delivered for me tomorrow. I'm going to rebuild the frame, expand it. First though, I'd like to take a look inside the house to see what needs to be done. See what I can repair."

April's blood began to boil with Will's first words. "You sure are confident you're going to win. What if you don't? Are you going to tear down everything you've built?"

"I'm taking a gamble, Miss Wilde." He removed his hat, swiped his head with his arm, and replaced the hat. "But it's a gamble I'm at ease with. If I lose, it all stays. If I win, it'll be ready for my family when they arrive."

The man was impossible. She wanted to tell him he wasn't stepping one foot inside her door. Sheriff Moss had told her she didn't have to let him. Told him to stay in the barn. But she knew better than anyone how drafty the cabin was. She had no other more vivid memory than of the last night of her mother's life, when Sarah was shivering so badly and April could do nothing about it. But there had never been money for luxuries, like new walls, so the chill had remained.

That didn't stop April from having a mental wish list of things that could use repair; the floorboards beneath the stove needed shoring, the shutters needed resealing, there were two leaks in the roof. So if Will Caulder wanted to spend his own money and his own time making things better, why would she stop him? "If you lose, whatever you've completed stays?"

"Stays. Can I have a look inside?"

"All right," she offered. "After morning chores are done. So I can keep an eye on you. I'll make a list of things that could use fixing."

Will nodded and forced his gaze away from April and on to the orange and red sunset. He *was* taking a risk in sinking all the money he'd won from Lyonel Sims into the farm. But as he'd told April, it was a risk he was willing to take. He needed a better home for his mother and sister, needed a larger home. While he was waiting for his family to arrive—and for the judge to set a hearing—he planned on adding two new sleeping rooms and expanding the kitchen and living area. And if he failed to win the claim, well—he glanced at April again, finding it difficult to keep his eyes from her even though the sunset was spectacular—the Wilde girls had lived long enough in the comfortless cabin.

The next morning Will set a plank of wood in place and picked up a hammer, determined to concentrate.

The cabin consisted of two bedrooms, the cooking area along one long wall, the rough-hewn eating table, and a cozy living area beside the hearth. April was seated near that hearth, in the rocker he'd occupied

while she'd tended his head. She was mending a pile
of clothes. But even from the kitchen, several feet
away, where he was replacing the boards to sturdy the
cast-iron stove, he could smell her fragrant feminine
scent lingering in the air.

This despite wood ash from the stove, May's bread
rising on the window sill, and the apples June was
peeling at the table.

He wouldn't have believed it. But his nose wasn't
lying. Hadn't lied to him yet. He could smell the subtle
flowery scent of her; the same alluring fragrance that
had set him on his heels the first night he'd met her
in the barn. The same aroma he'd enjoyed yesterday
during their meeting with Claymore and again after
he'd caught up to her on his way back from town.
Earlier today, she'd walked him around the house,
pointing out areas that needed attention. She'd finally
left him to his repairs while she moved to the other
side of the room. But she was still too close. And he
was still too distracted by that scent, and by everything
else about her.

He'd reminded himself last night while lying awake
in the chilled barn that he couldn't bend. He'd replayed the events of the afternoon, how, after meeting
with Mr. Dortch to buy supplies, he'd intentionally
ridden Tate hard to catch up to her. Because he wanted
her company. And how he'd deliberately teased her
just so he could take pleasure in her fiery replies.

Mostly, he'd replayed their visit to Cirrus Claymore's office. He should have stayed out of her dispute with the attorney. But even he knew that would
have been impossible. April didn't deserve to be ma-
nipulated the way Claymore was trying to manipulate
her. No woman did. Which was how Will eventually
rationalized his behavior.

He'd have come to any woman's rescue. And he'd have been worried if he wasn't attracted to April. She was stunning. Everything he could ask for in a woman, in a wife. And he wanted that: a woman like her, a small piece of land to hoe, animals to tend, crops to harvest—even children to raise. Once his family was settled, his world would be complete if he found someone like her.

Like her, not *her*.

Someone just as pretty, just as fiery, and someone who smelled just as good. He'd be able to concentrate on all those sweet things then. But in the meanwhile, *this* woman wasn't going to be his wife. And she stood in the way of his claiming the land. He had to put his attraction aside and start ignoring her.

Even so, he glanced her way. She was wearing a pale brown day dress again; so different from the pretty blue jacket and yellow skirt she had worn yesterday. And her gold hair was tight in a bun at the back of her head. At present she was deftly threading a needle, her gaze steadfast on the black skirt she was stitching.

He wondered how many times she had dressed in pretty clothing. How much pleasure she'd had over the years. He still didn't know how long her mother had been dead, but he was beginning to think it had been a long time. And that April had carried a heavy burden for far too long.

"There." June jerked him from his speculative thoughts. "I've cored enough apples for two cobblers. One for us and . . ." She blushed scarlet.

"One for Tobias Reeves," May finished with a friendly girlish smirk.

"Aren't you still sweet on Luke Hart?" April teased.

June lifted her chin defiantly. "I'm sweet on neither.

Tobias just asked me if I could bake and dared me to show him when I said I could. And Luke, well Luke is just a blacksmith. I couldn't possibly settle for a plain ol' blacksmith."

"June Wilde," April blustered. "What a snobbish thing to say."

"I'm just being practical, April," June countered. "I'm going to marry a wealthy man." She eyed both May and April, then added passionately, "One of us has to if we're ever going to be more than dirt poor. Especially if Mr. Caulder kicks us out of our home."

Will watched the three of them turn their gazes his way. He felt like he'd been punched in the gut. Especially when June burst into tears.

"Now June," May soothed. She took June into her arms and patted her back.

April rose from the rocker and left her mending on the seat. "June, dear, we aren't going anywhere," she said as she approached her sisters. "Everything will be fine."

She glared at Will. He turned away.

He received a curt missive from a messenger the following morning at the same time April did. He opened his while standing in front of the barn door. She read hers from the porch, chewed her bottom lip and glanced down at him.

Judge Claymore had set the time for their hearing at three o'clock that afternoon. Tucking the notice into his shirt pocket where the deed was still harbored, he turned his attention back to the fresh stack of wood. He stacked ten planks on top of the wheelbarrow and rolled them to the far side of the house where he had already started enlarging the frame.

Once out of April's sight, he stopped, removed his

hat and looked heavenward. The sun was still low in the sky. It was hours till three o'clock.

You led me here. I know You did. I've got the family coming and I've sunk every penny You gave me into supplies for this place. Now I'm asking You to see this thing through. Make it short and sweet. And give the Wilde sisters a new—better—place to go. None of us can take much more of this.

April fretted all the way to town. She wanted an answer. Wanted someone to strike Will Caulder down, make him leave. Anything that would prevent her from facing Judge Claymore so he could rule against her.

She had no desire to suffer such humiliation. To stand before someone so prejudiced against her and plead for her home.

And she didn't deserve it!

There had to be a way to make Will leave. Why couldn't he just realize he was wrong and go away? Or Sheriff Moss run him out of town?

She received no answer on the wind.

She sighed wearily and steered Solomon into the larger town of Denver where the hearing would be held.

"Look at all those people!" June suddenly exclaimed. "My word, all of Ruley is here. And they're all looking at us."

April forgot to breathe. June wasn't exaggerating. It did look as if every person who lived in and around Ruley had gathered outside the Denver courthouse. People stood about in small little groups. And they were all watching the girls' buckboard plod down the road.

How had word spread so quickly about the hearing?

Or that it was this afternoon? And by whom, she wanted to know. Moreover, why had everyone decided it was their business to attend?

She closed her eyes and forced air into her lungs, forced herself to stay calm.

"April, are you all right?" May asked from beside her. "You're so pale. Do you think you can get through this? We'll leave. We don't need the farm. You can turn around if you want." May touched April's arm tenderly.

"I . . . I'm fine," April replied and demanded herself to believe it. She was not going to allow her adversaries to win. Surely they were all hoping she would do something they could ridicule.

Well, she wasn't about to give them the satisfaction of seeing her faint, or turn tail and run. She'd face them all down, and never show them how much she hurt inside.

Fighting back bitter bile that lodged in her throat, she took a deep breath. They were *not* going to win. Not Will and not the multitude staring her down. She would show them all.

She brought Solomon to a halt far enough from the civic building so that she could exit the wagon without anyone being too close. She didn't need to trip and fall only to listen to their snickers.

Once she was safely on her feet, she smoothed the stark black skirt and jacket she wore. The outfit had been her mother's. She vaguely remembered Sarah wearing it to a town meeting months before her death. April had carefully finished sprucing it up only yesterday while Will was repairing the kitchen floorboards. While she'd sat in the rocker and thought how natural it felt to have a man in the house, fixing things.

Now yesterday seemed so long ago, a surreal dream that had never taken place.

"Don't worry, April," June offered as she hurried to April's side and linked her arm in hers. "We'll be with you the entire time. Why, I can't imagine that Judge Claymore will do anything but scold Mr. Caulder for putting us through this. And if he dares try to give our house to that man, why I'll give the judge a piece of my mind. I'll—"

"June, please," May broke in. "It's not going to come to that. I'm sure the judge will be very fair. He knows as well as we do that Mr. Caulder's claim is foul."

"Yes, of course he does." April's voice sounded distant to her own ears.

"And even if he does give our farm away—if we're living under the stars after today—we'll always be together." May claimed April's hand, smiled and squeezed.

"Oh," June sobbed. "Do you really think we might have to sleep outside? It's so cold out already. And it's only autumn. I really can't—"

"June!" May cried. She tossed her a warning glare.

June sniffed and squared her shoulders. "Yes, at least we'll always be together. No matter what. And remember what Mama told us, April, just before she died. A flower's . . ."

. . . bloom will be most brilliant after the rain.

April let the words roll through her mind and across her tongue. She had said them many times over the years. Had stood firm with them, claimed them. She was glad June had thought to encourage her with them now, even if she thought she was drowning.

There was little else she could do but face the crowd and Judge Claymore, so she lifted herself as tall as she could, patted the hat that held her hair up, and with her sisters following, marched down the wooden boardwalk. She knew her cheeks were tinged red when she was forced to bypass a detachment of soldiers and their two Indian scouts waiting outside the telegraph, and the merchants who had stepped outside to observe the goings-on.

The horde from Ruley buzzed louder as she approached. Then a hush fell over them. She wanted to ask them why they thought they had the right to watch her destruction, why they weren't home doing better things with their time. But she pretended to ignore them instead; Lou Dortch, owner of the mercantile she sold her jam to, the Guetuen twins, Hans and Ben, who were lazy good-for-nothings usually found in Ruley's saloon, and Mrs. Layburn, who should be tending her honey bees.

Pastor Johnson was even there. He stepped forward to give her a reassuring pat on the shoulder, before he blended in with the crowd again.

When April saw Sheriff Moss, Will beside him, she nearly stopped in her tracks. Only with effort did she keep her pace, but she tossed them both a withering glare she hoped conveyed her loathing.

Will stepped into her path. "After you." He extended his hand gallantly for her to enter the civic building. "No reason why we can't enter the courthouse together."

April knew of several reasons, but before she could rebut Will's remarks, she heard, "I'll escort Miss Wilde into the courthouse, Caulder."

April's gaze swiveled to Cirrus, leather case in hand. He was pushing his way through the crowd.

"Move aside, move aside," he barked.

The crowd began to drone again in anticipation

while Cirrus circled April's arm with his hand. "Miss Wilde," he said with a touch of contempt as he caught her up in his quick pace. He pushed open the heavy door.

"Did you talk to your father?" she asked. "Do you have any idea how he feels about the claim?"

"No and no," Cirrus stated coldly.

"What should I do?" she tried again. "What should I expect?"

He led her through a pair of hardwood doors and into a wide open and airy room converted into a court-house because of the growing population and crime. He pulled her down the aisle lined with hardwood chairs, through a half-swinging door and to a large table. Holding a chair, he waited for her to be seated. Then he bent over her with a sneer. "You should have thought of these questions when you were in my office, *April*. But you were sure you didn't need any time alone with me, remember?"

April wondered if things could get any worse. "I apologize if you thought I was being rude, Mr. Claymore. That wasn't my intention."

"What was your intention, other than slighting me again?" Cirrus pursed his flat lips before he sighed. "Just answer my questions when I call you to the stand," he told her. "And the Judge's questions if he has any. And remember, he is the judge today—*not* my father."

She nodded as he took the seat beside her. She glanced around to make sure May and June were seated behind her. Then another commotion made her look across the room to where Will sat at an identical table.

"Don't look at him," Cirrus admonished.

"Why not?"

He sighed again. April thought he was acting like a petulant child. "Because it's not wise to look at your opponent. The judge might read something into it. You'd have known that as well had you met with me in private."

"Oh." April sat back in the chair and looked straight ahead. "I'm sorry then. I should have realized." And yet she wanted to tell him that if she hadn't been so concerned about his behavior, if she'd felt she could trust him even a smidgen, she would have met with him in private.

"Cirrus, dear."

April pivoted toward the voice, new dread filling her as she watched Sadie Claymore walk over to her son and squeeze his cheeks. "I'm sure you'll do fine today, son, even—" She let her gaze fall on April— "Even if you don't prevail. You know your father must do what's right for the community."

Cirrus's face reddened. "Mother, this is not the time."

Sadie faded into the crowd.

"Stand up," Cirrus ordered April then. He took her arm again, roughly, and began to pull her to her feet as Judge Claymore entered a side door. Everyone else crowding into the room behind them did the same. After the judge was seated at a table facing the audience, they all returned to their seats.

April tried to ignore the pit in her stomach. She had never been in a courtroom setting, didn't have an inkling of what took place. And yet her surroundings fascinated her. If it weren't for the fact that her life was on the line she would have been enthralled by the adventure of it all.

"Now then," Judge Claymore began. "Are all the parties present?"

"Yes, Your Honor," Cirrus shouted, rising halfway out of his chair.

"Yes, Your Honor," Will added loudly.

The judge was a robust man, rounder than he was tall, with brooding eyes beneath bushy brows and a sagging chin that wobbled when he spoke. He leaned back in his high-backed squeaky leather chair and laced his hands together, staring at Will.

April had one memory of the man from when her mother died; he'd helped dig Sarah's grave in the frozen ground, then carried her mother's blanket-wrapped body outside and laid her to rest. Afterward, he'd returned to the cabin and knelt down in front of April. "You want to come live with me and Mrs. Claymore?" he'd asked.

She'd shaken her head, young and terrified and distrustful.

He'd nodded and stood again. "The missus will be by to check on you then," he'd said as he left. And had it been only Mrs. Claymore, and not her son, things might have been so different.

"And who are you?" the judge challenged Will now.

"I'm Will Caulder. I hold the deed to the land the Wilde sisters are living on." Will rubbed the bandage covering his cut. "A deed giving me ownership of that land. Signed and witnessed."

The audience collectively gasped. April pulled her gaze away from him and stared at her shaking hands.

"Hush, all of you." The judge's bellow rang throughout the room. "Or I'll toss all of you out of my court."

"Your Honor," Cirrus began then and stood. "Mr. Caulder is in error and we'll prove to the court that the farm April Wilde and her sisters live on has always been theirs, and that this man—" He pointed to Will. "Is a fortune-seeker, preying on three innocent girls."

April listened to Cirrus's statement with relief. At least he *was* going to defend her. But his words caused more collective grumbling in the crowd, and one person snorted loudly. April knew immediately that it was Sadie Claymore.

April groaned, earning a warning glance from Cirrus.

"As I was saying, Your Honor," the attorney went on. "We'll prove—"

"Let's get to the point," Claymore interrupted. He eyed Cirrus and Will. "I've read the complaint. Where's this deed?"

He had no patience, April saw that right away. He wasn't going to listen to her tale of hardship and woe. He was going to be straight-laced, take one look at the signed deed and award Will her home.

Someone coughed, making April aware of how quiet the courtroom had become. Will's footsteps were loud as he approached the judge's table.

The judge abruptly took the piece of paper from Will's hand, eyed Will with sternness and put his spectacles on. Then he began to study the deed.

April's hands grew clammy. She rubbed them together.

"Stop that," Cirrus scolded again.

April immediately halted her movement, but not without a questioning scowl. She wasn't going to put up with Cirrus treating her so rudely much longer.

"Well, it's signed," Percy Claymore told the audience. "By Justus A. Wilde."

"Yes, Your Honor." Will placed his hands behind his back. "And dated and witnessed by two men."

"All drunk, Judge." Cirrus stood again. "We profess

that Mr. Wilde would have never gambled away the property his daughters have called home all their lives if he was in his right mind. Therefore, the document you hold could not possibly—"

The judge held up his hand for Cirrus to be silent. He leaned forward, looked Will in the eye and lifted a menacing brow. "I knew Justus Wilde," he said as if Will were the only person in the room. "He could hold his spirits, that's for certain. How drunk was he?" His mouth hung like a horseshoe as he waited for Will's answer.

"I didn't know Justus Wilde, Judge," Will replied. "But for the two times we played cards. I'd say he was drunker the second time than the first. But when he wagered his land I gave him the chance to back out. I did so because he was drunk. I didn't want to take advantage of him."

The judge pondered his answer. "I see. And Wilde went ahead with the bet?"

Will nodded. "He thought he'd won."

"Well then, if he knew what he was doing—"

"He died that same night!" April jumped from her seat. The crowd gasped at her outburst, but she didn't care. She had to do something fast.

"April, sit down," Cirrus hissed.

April ignored him. "Justus Wilde couldn't have been in his right mind. He died."

Another hush fell over the room. Judge Claymore stared at her with one eye closed and one gray brow lifted. "Miss—"

"She's sorry, Your Honor," Cirrus was quick to say.

"No. No, sir. Your Honor. I'm not." Not if her outburst served to stop him from giving her land to Will Caulder.

The judge's frown remained and both brows knitted.

He began to drum his fingers against the tabletop. "Miss Wilde, how old are you now?" he asked then.

"What does my age—"

"Answer him," Cirrus whispered harshly.

"Nineteen, sir. Your Honor."

"And your sisters?"

She glanced at May and June seated directly behind her. Both wore anxious expressions. They held each other's hands.

"Seventeen and eighteen, Your Honor."

The jurist sighed heavily and sat back in his chair. After a moment of dead silence, when it was evident everyone was holding their breaths, he said, "It's been a long time since your pa left and your mama died. Very well. I want more proof. I want the witnesses found, affidavits signed or them personally brought here."

The crowd buzzed and Judge Claymore pounded his gavel. "This hearing will reconvene in two weeks." He stood and strode through the side door while the courtroom exploded into noise.

"What does this mean?" April turned to Cirrus as people all around them rose in a squall of gibbering. "What's happening?"

Cirrus glared at her as he shoved papers back into his briefcase. "He wants more proof. He's postponed his decision for two weeks. He'll have Sheriff Moss contact the sheriff in Cripple Creek and try to track down the two witnesses who signed the deed. He wants them to testify."

"Yes, but until then?" May and June were now beside her, listening intently. April didn't know what to make of the judge's decision.

Cirrus paused to consider her. "It appears your outburst worked. You can stay on the property."

May and June sighed with relief.

"And Mr. Caulder?"

"The judge didn't clarify," Cirrus answered. "Which means, I suppose, Caulder can, too."

April glanced over to see Will seated at the desk staring into space. Was he as shocked as she was?

"We were lucky, April," Cirrus said harshly then. "The judge could have thrown you out of court for what you did. It was childish. Now maybe you'll begin to listen to me." He paused with a short sigh. "I only want what's best for you."

April wasn't sure how to respond. She didn't feel as if she'd been childish at all. Her "outburst" had worked. And she'd do it again if she had to. But she didn't want to upset Cirrus more, so she held her tongue and followed him from the room. All the while she kept wondering what she should hope for now; that the two men who witnessed her father's betrayal could be found? Or that they couldn't?

Chapter Six

Will waited for the crowd to disperse before he stood to leave. He had given Sheriff Moss the descriptions of Pedro Rodriguez and Lyonel Sims and told him the name of the saloon where they had played cards. Now he was forced to wait.

For two more weeks.

And his family should arrive shortly thereafter. He was still stunned that Claymore had put the outcome on hold. His evidence was more than enough to render a ruling. But Will had seen the tender look that had crossed the judge's face when he looked at April. Was there a possibility Claymore would side with her just because he felt sorry for her?

Having been around now for a few days, he'd begun to hear the stories circulating about the eldest Wilde sister. He knew she wasn't well liked. April herself had hinted to the fact that she didn't need any more trouble. Will knew now it had something to do with April refusing Sadie Claymore's benevolence years before. Why such a silly thing was still shadowing her was beyond him. But based on the animosity toward her, he'd concluded Judge Claymore would quickly rule in his favor. He'd apparently been wrong. And it was now obvious the judge didn't feel quite the same as his wife and the rest of the folks in Ruley.

Now Will was faced with another two weeks of uncertainty.

He hoped, during that time, the sheriff would find Rodriguez and Simms. And afterwards, the judge would have no choice but to rule in his favor. In the meanwhile, he'd keep refurbishing the house and renew his resolve to keep his distance from April Wilde. Another two weeks of seeing her every day was going to be hard to take. If he wanted to keep his sanity.

There wasn't much to the farm except the house and barn. Most of the property was untilled, unfenced open range. There weren't any cattle and little livestock other than the two horses, milk cow, and noisy chickens. But there was a fenced pasture, an area where the horses were put out to graze and a round paddock.

When the wind picked up two days later and Will was forced to abandon his efforts at finishing the house's west wall, he headed out to secure pasture fence posts instead. Fall weather in Colorado was as fickle as any female; snowy one day, bright and warm the next. He pretty much didn't mind anything God's nature could muster up except the bone-numbing wind. And he'd have liked to call it a day, head back to the barn and relative warmth. But he couldn't—wouldn't—until April returned from the river.

She'd passed him on her way to the water awhile

ago, a burlap sack in hand. They hadn't said a word to each other since Judge Claymore had postponed the hearing. But they were battling nonetheless. He'd catch her watching him sometimes with those green eyes of hers glistening with anger, and something else he wished he could define but hadn't quite been able to put his finger on. And she'd caught him staring at her once or twice—maybe more—as well.

He kept to himself as much as he could, continued to sleep in the barn, continued to take his meals from May. June was the one who had become a little more cordial. She'd even sat with him for a time last night while he was gazing at the clear starry sky.

But her oldest sister refused to give him the time of day. Since he didn't want to give her any excuse she could use against him in court—or think he couldn't weather a little cold wind—he turned up the collar of his coat, tugged on the sleeves, and kept staking fence-post, waiting for her return.

April finished plucking the chicken in record time. She had always hated the task, but today, thinking about Will Caulder made it easier. She only had to picture plucking him instead of the dead bird. The feathers had flown off. She'd hoped, after Judge Claymore's ruling in court the other day, he'd find another place to stay. He'd known he wasn't welcome at the farm. She couldn't be more unfriendly if she tried. But much to her consternation, he was still pestering them with his presence. And he seemed quite content with himself. More than once she'd considered ending her decision to feed him just so he'd have to find another place to eat. She'd never been under any obligation to be generous. And in her mind, the situation didn't lend itself to loving thy neighbor. But, she'd reasoned he'd never asked to be fed in the first place, so that wouldn't have motivated him to leave. Nothing seemed to motivate him to leave. In fact, with each new day he seemed to be more firmly rooted at the farm than the day before.

Which caused April a considerable amount of anxiety. Caulder already acted as if he owned the place. He was more than half done enlarging the exterior of the house. He worked late into the night mending and fixing everything he could.

She'd been caught watching him several times. He'd straighten from digging a hole to wipe his brow, or to grab a new post, and she'd have to quickly turn away.

Not that she hadn't felt him watching her, too. Last night she'd been kneeling by her mother's grave on the hill west of the house, having a much-needed heart-to-heart talk about faith and storms and blooms and spring, when she'd turned toward the barn and saw him leaning against the door. Just this morning, she'd been hanging laundry. She'd been able to feel his eyes burning into her back. When she'd turned, she'd seen him on the top rung of the repaired ladder, the hammer in his hand forgotten as he stared at her.

April admitted he made her jittery. Made her scatterbrained. Which was why she'd forgotten all about tonight's supper. The bird should have been boiling on the stove by now. Supper would be late and it was Will Caulder's fault.

Instead of concentrating on her chores, she was always trying to come up with new ways to get rid of him—and all the while she'd watch him pound spikes with his muscular arms or carry fence posts on his wide shoulders. She'd tried not to watch the way his light-brown hair whipped in the wind, or how his shirt strained against his back as he wiped perspiration from his brow, but it never worked.

April hurried now, furious with herself for letting her mind wander with thoughts of him yet again. The man was a nuisance. A handsome one, but an enemy on her own turf.

She ignored the wind whipping the copse of choke-cherry, and she stuffed the featherless chicken back into the burlap sack before kneeling down on the riverbank to wash. The frigid water and air stung her arms, making her teeth chatter. That was Will Caulder's fault, too. If she'd remembered to pluck the bird earlier after she returned from cleaning Cirrus's office for the first time—

She heard it then, the eerie cry, the yip and bark.

April swiveled sharply, fear slicing through her, but she couldn't see the coyote anywhere. Then another cry floated on the wind; this one from the opposite direction. She turned to her right, scanning the landscape, and saw it, tongue lagging, staring right at her from twenty feet away.

How could she have been so foolish? she scolded herself. The chicken's scent, blown about by the wind, had drawn the coyote right to her. She darted her gaze to the left again and saw the second mangy animal on the edge of the copse. He took a step toward her. She hoped there were only two, and yet two was two too many. Slowly rising to her feet, she kept her gaze on both predators and picked up the burlap bag, deciding to toss it as far as she could, hoping the coyotes would rush for the bag.

When the animal on her right took another step closer to her she heaved the bag. To her amazement both animals gave the bag a cursory glance before returning their attention to her. It was obvious the chicken's scent was still on the ground in front of her. The coyote by the copse raised his head and howled. His partner yipped. April stepped backwards into the river, felt the icy water invade the soles of her boots and freeze her feet. She was going to have to plunge into the current. Escape—if she didn't freeze to death first—to the bank on the opposite side, and hope the animals didn't follow.

But just as she'd made up her mind to do so, she heard a gunshot explode in the air. The noise startled her, made her stumble back another pace before she caught herself. The pair of coyotes startled as well. And then Will was running toward her, gun raised.

"Haaa! Haaa!" he shouted.

The animals bolted. Will came to a hard splashing stop in the water in front of April, his back to her as he scanned the landscape for the predators.

"You okay?" His chest rose with exertion from his run.

"I . . . I think . . . yes," April gasped. "They're gone?"

"Yeah, they took off." He stepped onto the bank, his gun still poised for attack. April sloshed out of the water behind him, shivering from cold and shock.

"You okay?" he asked again.

"They must have smelled the chicken. I was so stupid. I wasn't paying attention. I can't believe . . ."

He spun around to face her, his gaze intense, and after a brief moment he wrapped his warm palm along the curve of her neck and jaw. "Shhh. It's all right now. It's over."

His thumb slid easily across her chilled skin. April swallowed and stared up at him, the heat of him warming her, the calmness in him drawing her. She had never—ever—relied on another person for her safety before. Never—ever—known such a luxury existed. She didn't quite know what to make of Will charging to her rescue, to know that without his assistance she could still be fighting off the coyotes' advances.

It was a raw feeling knowing she wasn't alone, knowing she could rely—

April caught her thoughts and nearly choked. Her *rescuer* was trying to steal her land. How could she forget so easily? She backed away from his hand and felt the icy wind sting the area he had cradled. "I need to get supper started," she said, more to herself than to him. "I need to find the chicken."

She began to trek up the small slope toward the clearing where she had tossed the burlap bag. She glanced left and right, making certain the coyote were gone. Behind her, she heard Will's boots crunching dead leaves and earth as he followed her. But she couldn't look back. She couldn't. If she did, April knew she might just run right into his arms.

"April! Mr. Caulder!"

"Get out of those boots," April said to Will before they'd reached the porch. May and June had run out to meet them halfway home.

"We heard the shots! What happened?"

"Leave them outside and come into the house." Her words were clipped, her tone harsh. She ignored her sisters and tossed the burlap bag by the front door, bending down to unfasten the laces of her own wet boots. Then she drew in her breath as she worked her frozen feet from the leather.

Oh, she hurt. She couldn't stop from shivering. Her feet stung, and her heart—her heart stung worse.

"April?" May said again, this time drawing her attention.

"I was almost attacked by a pair of coyotes," April told them. "Mr. Caulder scared them off. Stoke the fire, one of you. Mr. Caulder is wet. And please find him some dry socks."

She was babbling, she knew it, but she had to keep busy. If she stopped to think. . . . "I'll warm you some milk," she added to Will without daring to look at him. "There's a blanket near the hearth. I'll get that for you, too."

She finished peeling off her socks with a sharp intake of breath. May and June had already disappeared. And then Will was beside her, taking her wrist in his hand and drawing her around to face him.

"You're in worse shape than I am. You need the fire. I'll be fine."

"No. I insist." She couldn't be beholden to him. She couldn't. "Please go inside and warm up. Get dry. I . . ."

"April." The sound of her name on his lips silenced her. She could feel the weight of his hand holding her wrist. She slowly lifted her gaze from the wooden flooring and looked into his eyes. Penetrating eyes that seemed to see into her very being.

For a moment they just stared at one another, and then . . . then April watched Will lean forward slightly. His gaze dropped to her mouth. She swallowed, and waited—until he abruptly backed away.

"Go inside," he ordered. "Sit down in front of the fireplace and don't move until you're dry and warm."

She quickly lowered her gaze, heat radiating through her. Did he know what he had just done to her? What she thought he was going to do to her? "You—"

"I'm right behind you."

She nodded, too numb from fierce cold and sudden heat to do anything else.

Later that night Will lay in the loft with the extra quilt May had given him tucked around him, and listened to the silence outside. The wind had died at sunset. The coyotes had moved on. The sky outside was illuminated by a full harvest moon, and there wasn't a cloud around. All was calm again at the farm.

He couldn't say the same inside his head.

Today's adventure with April had stirred in him things he had fought hard to keep unstirred. When he'd heard the coyote, his first thought was to get to April. When he'd seen her backed into the water, one predator on each side of her, his heart had pounded like never before. He would have run barefoot across shards of glass to save her. And then . . . her skin had felt so soft and warm beneath his palm, her wrist so fragile and cold within his grasp. How she had ever managed to survive in such a harsh environment, on her own, while raising two younger sisters was beyond him.

And yet even in the face of danger she'd remained calm, tried to put him first, argued with him until he had practically forced her into the house. They had sat for nearly an hour in front of the fire, trying to get warm, while May and June brought them steaming milk. June had jabbered the entire time, helping to ease a curtain of tension that was so thick it was hard to part. April didn't look at him, she merely stared into the fire's flame. And the one time he'd tried to talk to her she'd pretended she didn't hear him.

When May had announced supper was ready, Will had taken the offering with him to the barn. The hot, thick chicken stew and dumplings had kept him warm as night closed in, when the only things that remained restless were the horses and his mind's wanderings. Mind wanderings he was determined would not reach his heart, even if he knew himself for a liar.

Chapter Seven

He rode in at noon three days later, a wild mustang harnessed behind his horse. April hadn't talked to him since the incident at the river, didn't want to talk to him. But that didn't mean she hadn't seen him. He was hard to ignore.

She'd known this morning when she woke that he was gone. She'd wondered when he'd left, why she hadn't heard him leave—and when he'd be back. Now she knew he'd been out chasing the same horses she dreamed of taming.

His own horse, Tate, was a sleek black and well behaved. On occasion, when no one was watching, she'd slip Tate a bit of dried apple and wonder what it would feel like to be on his back, racing through the meadows. Since she knew a thing or two about horseflesh, she knew Will took good care of Tate.

Will also sat him well, bringing him to a fast, hard

halt in the paddock, while his attention was centered on the mustang. She could see Will's powerful thigh muscles contracting, his feet in the stirrups steering his horse.

"Easy does it, boy," he said as the mustang tried to stomp his way loose of the rope around his neck. Will kept his hands firmly on the corded line and tossed his leg over the saddle, then slid from Tate's back. The black backed away from the paddock. Will dropped the lead rope and closed the gate, leaving the mustang to buck and kick in the corral while he climbed onto the bottom rung to watch.

April knew the mustang. He led the wild herd as they roamed the land, evading even the Arapahoe. He was a rust color with white socks and a long scar across his chest. His mane was mangy and his coat dirty. He pranced around the paddock with angry indignation. And yet he wasn't the only one who was surprised he'd been caught. She wouldn't have thought catching mustangs was one of Will's aspirations.

With a perplexed frown she left the porch and walked across the dormant prairie grass. He was standing on the bottom rung of the fence, peering over the rail. She stepped up beside him. "What are your plans for him?" she asked, nodding toward the beautiful animal.

Beneath his hat she saw Will's gaze shift her way. She could tell he was surprised she'd joined him. She was surprised herself. Since the fiasco at the river she'd purposely steered clear of him, and she'd sensed he'd tried to do the same.

"Tame him, train him. Him and many others." His tone was casual. He rubbed the healing cut on his brow. "Then I'll breed the best."

April's distress deepened. Not only was he trying to steal her land, he was also trying to steal her dream.

She was the one who wanted to raise horses, breed them sleeker and faster and smarter. She'd waited years to allow herself the pleasure of considering her dream might soon take shape—only to have, that very night, Will walk into her life. Was that to be stripped of her as well?

She sighed silently, knowing she couldn't worry about the loss of one wild mustang. If she kept her land, there'd be more. She'd start with her mare. And if she didn't win, it wouldn't matter.

Still, she stared at the prancing beast now, refusing to look at his trapper. "I came out here to thank you," she blurted. "For helping me at the river the other day. I never did properly tell you how much I appreciated your help."

Will slid down from the fence and faced her. April followed, then wished she hadn't. He was much taller than she, intimidating.

"I'm usually not so dense. I should have been paying more attention," she added.

"It could have happened to anyone," he interrupted.

"No, not if you're careful," she argued. "And I wasn't. Which is dangerous out here. I know better."

"April, anyone can be blindsided." The sound of her name on his lips made her insides flutter.

"Well, I—"

"Don't be so hard on yourself. Look at this stallion." He motioned to the animal. "He wasn't expecting me to capture him. Even he was blindsided."

April saw his point. She half-smiled. If the mustang could be caught. . . .

"I'm just glad I was around to help," Will added. He grinned, lopsided, and April's heart hitched. She'd never seen him smile before. Not like this. There was so much animosity between them, there'd never been a moment for anything else.

She nodded. "I wish there'd been no need." Or did she? Their few moments together, during and after the scare, had been the most extraordinary April had ever experienced. She wouldn't give them back if she could.

She shook her head to clear it, fighting the reflection. "I wanted you to know I'm grateful. You didn't have to come to my aid. It was too cold to work. You shouldn't have been out there in the first place."

"But I was." Will's gaze narrowed, his blue eyes intense. "Perhaps just for that reason."

His words jolted her. Had Will been deliberately placed in the field so he could hear the coyote? So he could rescue her?

"Perhaps so you could reward me."

She sucked in her breath. Had she heard right? He was staring right at her, probing her for a response. What kind, she wondered. Was he baiting her to see if she was weakening? Was he trying to find out if she would be receptive to more moments like their few on the porch? Was he trying to find out if she'd let him kiss her? Or was he expecting her to reward him by giving him her land?

Quickly losing her battle for calmness, she decided not to answer. She headed for the house instead.

"April?" Will called after her.

What was it about her name when he said it that made her heart pump faster? She paused and swung around to face him.

"You, ah . . . June told me you trained Solomon and Samson. I could use another hand with the mustang. Interested?"

She wanted to say yes. It would be wonderful to

work with the rust. She wanted to say no more—and mean it. She compromised, declined his offer with a quick shake of her head, and continued on her way. But with every step she could feel her heart tear more. By the time she reached the porch, she needed to use the post just to steady herself. Behind her she could hear Will talking to the mustang. He had evidently dismissed her from thought just as quickly as she'd turned him down. Giving in to her best effort otherwise, she turned to watch him entering the corral. His corded shoulders lifted, his large hands reached out to the horse. He used a soothing tone as he closed the space between them.

Envy surged through her frame. What she wouldn't give to be in the paddock with him. To be part of his effort to gentle the rust. More so, what she wouldn't give to be the recipient of his gentle tone, and to feel the caress of his caring hands. Of course her desire had nothing to do with the man himself. Just one *like* Will; a man who tackled things with earnest. One who risked his own life for others. One who was caring and patient.

April gripped the rail tighter. Until Will's arrival she'd never thought a man like him existed. She had learned long ago that men tarnished dreams and tread heavily on hearts. She knew firsthand they were not to be trusted. And that a woman could never allow herself to fall for their lies like her mother had.

But now she saw there were a few—at least one—who was different. And if there was one maybe there were two. Maybe she could find someone *like* Will, someone who wanted to help her tend the farm, who had a passion for horses. Who was better than Will because he wasn't after her land, her home.

One thing was certain, if she was able to keep the

farm, and May and June did leave, she now realized she was going to be awfully lonely.

Will took the hardy slap to his back in stride, listened to the stranger's encouragement, and kept on drinking his sarsaparilla. He had been in town for a couple hours, after inventorying his supplies and deciding he needed more. He needed time away from the farm as well. Away from April.

A week had passed since Judge Claymore had put his claim on hold, a week during which he had saturated himself in rebuilding and repairs. He still had plenty to occupy his time, but being around April every day was wearing on him. The woman had a way about her that beckoned him to stop whatever he was doing and watch her. Not wanting to be too conspicuous, he'd steal glimpses of her instead; as she daily trekked from house to barn and back, when she was sweeping the porch or visiting the grave on the hillside. Twice he'd entered the barn to find her humming a song. When she saw him, she'd immediately stopped and left.

But as always her scent lingered, enticing him, intoxicating him. He certainly didn't need stronger drink to spin his head. April had done that without it. Which was why he was sitting in the saloon.

The men in the smoke-filled establishment had welcomed him roundly. Several had patted him on the back. A few had offered to buy him a shot of whiskey. He'd refused the liquor easily enough, but he needed allies until the claim was settled. So Will put up with the reception. Given because April Wilde had once tread on Sadie Claymore's toes. Which in turn had made them all feel as if she'd stung their collective pride. It failed to matter that Will was an outsider, that they could have been seeing things from April's perspective; he'd come to steal her land. And that they should have been rallying behind her instead.

Knowing they weren't didn't sit well with him. He found it hard to understand how they could be so against the Wilde sisters. But he'd decided there was as little he could do about changing their minds as there was about him changing his own.

"How about another sarsaparilla, Caulder?" he heard from behind him. "Seein's how you don't drink nothing else. Must want to keep yer wits about you so's you can beat those Wilde girls." The man guffawed at his own humor and several men joined him.

Will's stomach knotted. "I think I've had enough," he replied and meant it. He rose from the bar stool and started for the door. "I best be getting hom—back. See you around, gentlemen."

Outside, he took a breath of clean cool air and tried to shrug aside his agitation. Mr. Dortch should have his order pulled by now. He needed to head hom—

Home? The word stuck in his throat, sounded strange in his mind. Stranger still was the picture his mind conjured of the farm. Because standing in the center of his image, staring at the stunning Rockies, was a beautiful young woman with wheat-gold hair blowing in the breeze.

April.

The courtroom was noisier than ever the day the hearing resumed. April sat with her shoulders stiff and her eyes locked on the side door from which Judge Claymore would enter. She wrung her hands for the hundredth time as the clock struck the ninth hour. Behind her sat May, Edwin Talbot, and June. And behind them was the packed courtroom of curious observers.

Will was already seated behind a table just like hers. Cirrus had scowled when he finally arrived after she had already entered the room and claimed her seat.

"Impatient, are we?" he'd sneered. Since she'd made sure he wasn't in the office when she weekly went to clean it, and purposely dodged him when she saw him at church, she hadn't talked to him since the last hearing. And since she knew she was interfering with his plans to become more involved with her, she hadn't been certain he'd show up at all. Why, she'd asked herself, did he want to help her save her land? It was obvious his infatuation had turned to contempt. But either way, it struck her as odd that he was attempting to defend her.

She was oddly disappointed when he arrived. She was beginning to think she could do just as well persuading his father that she should prevail. She had finally realized that when he had asked all those years ago if she wanted to come live with him and Mrs. Claymore, that he was being kind. If only she'd known that then and not been so afraid of him.

But why did he have a wife and son who were so different from him? Still, she had to give Cirrus credit for his effort on her behalf.

"Here he comes," he said when the judge entered the room. He took her arm to help her rise.

Everyone else rose with them. When the judge pounded his gavel she startled, then cautioned herself against displaying emotion again. She couldn't afford any outbursts. She couldn't afford to alienate Judge Claymore.

Please, she silently prayed, *I've been asking You and asking You to make Will Caulder leave. I haven't heard one little whisper in reply. Are You up there? Please make him go away!*

"Well, it appears we've made some progress since we last met," the judge began, to pull her from her prayer. "As you know Miss Wilde, Mr. Caulder, I had Sheriff Moss search for the witnesses who signed their names to the deed Caulder has in his possession. I wanted to verify with them that the deed is real and valid. That there was no coercion on Caulder's part. And that Justus Wilde was in his right mind when and if he wagered his land."

She wasn't sure if she was supposed to acknowledge the judge's words or not so she stayed silent.

"It appears Sheriff Moss was able to locate one of the two witnesses."

He began to unfold a piece of paper as April's stomach lodged in her throat and the courtroom grew unbearably quiet.

"This here's the statement of Pedro Rodriguez. And in it he verifies what Mr. Caulder is claiming."

A collective gasp rose from the crowd. April's intake of breath was just as loud. She clamped down on her lip with her teeth, her head swimming.

"Mr. Rodriguez admits there was a card game, that Justus was drinking, and that he wagered his land. He states Mr. Caulder tried to get Justus to reconsider but Justus refused. And he says under oath that Mr. Caulder won the wager fair and square."

The crowd buzzed with discussion. Behind her April heard June burst into tears. She looked down at her hands, fighting the sick feeling in her soul. What would she do now? Where would she and her sisters go?

"Order! I'll have order in this court or boot the lot of you!" The judge's voice boomed throughout the room. The crowd was immediately silent.

"Now then, as I was saying," he went on, and April

fought away the pounding in her ears to hear him. "We have one witness who verifies Mr. Caulder's account. However, the Sheriff was unable to locate the second witness, Lyonel Sims." He paused, and April felt her heart slam against her chest.

"If the sheriff didn't feel there was any chance of tracking down the second witness, I'd be inclined to award the land based on the one witness's account. But . . ." He eyed first Will and then April. She held her breath. "But Sheriff's been tracking this fellow and thinks he'll be able to round him up by next week's end."

Again the crowd erupted.

"You're going to postpone it another week, Judge?" someone yelled.

"Don't you have enough evidence, Judge?" another voice shouted.

April watched the jurist's face turn blotchy red. His cheeks shook. "Out!" he roared. "Out, you miserable . . . ! I'll not have my court maligned like this!"

Sheriff Moss and one of his deputies darted from their seats and began herding the crowd from the room. Stunned, April watched as Cirrus told May and June to stay and then held the door open while the rest of the horde filed outside.

"I won't have disruptions, I tell you. I won't!" Judge Claymore shouted again when the last observer had departed. "Now then, as I was saying, since the Sheriff thinks he can track this man down, I'm going to wait a bit longer before I make my decision."

"Your Honor," Will called out and gained his feet. "I believe I've waited long enough, and so has Miss Wilde. This delay is not good for any of us. I'm asking you to decide now."

"Even if it means you'll lose, son?" Judge Claymore raised his bushy brow.

"Everything points my way, sir," he argued. "I have the deed. Pedro Rodriguez testified it was real."

Claymore's jowls sagged. "True enough, son. But it just wouldn't be fair for me to judge in your favor if Sims can be found soon. My ruling will last a lifetime."

April released the pent-up air in her lungs and watched as the judge reached for his gavel.

"I said we'll wait another week," he added. He stood and pounded his gavel, then ambled from the room.

April was too stunned to move. Another delay? She wasn't sure if she was angry or relieved. If she felt she'd been given a reprieve or merely another week of frustration before the inevitable happened.

At least, she concluded, she and her sisters had a roof over their heads for seven more days. She needed to be grateful for that much. She *was* grateful for that much. And now she had seven more days to help Will on his way.

She looked up as May and June scrambled around the swinging door to hug her. Then her gaze shifted to Will. She watched him rake a hand through his hair and kick a chair before he stormed out of the courthouse.

Chapter Eight

He walked into church purposely late that Sunday, wanting to make certain April was already seated before he made his appearance. He wasn't at all sure what she would do if she saw him invading this new area of her life. But he'd decided he needed to test the waters, build on the momentum of the townsfolk who'd rallied behind him. The pastor wasn't one of them, but Will hoped if the congregation was accepting, Pastor Johnson would come around. And perhaps he could convince one of his supporters to try and sway Judge Claymore.

His second reason was no less selfish; he planned to talk to Edwin Talbot, convince the man he needed to marry May sooner than later. Then he was going to find someone else who was head-over-heels for June and make the same suggestion.

With the two girls spoken for, April might welcome

her own suitor—someone like, like . . . well he'd
worry about that once the rest of his plan was in place.
Anyone except Cirrus Claymore. The idea was to take
away her need for the farm.

He stood at the back of the church while the wor-
shipers sang, then slipped around a couple and their
row of children, taking the seat beside them. The
woman's head snapped around when she noticed him.
She elbowed her husband, who frowned back at Will
with disapproval. Then a wiry younger version of the
man glared at Will. "You leave Miss April alone," he
hissed.

Will was surprised by the teen's venom. He thought
he'd seen him before, then remembered he lived on
the closest farm to the Wildes'. He was the first person
to show any loyalty to April. Which made Will wonder if he'd finally overstepped his bounds. Maybe his
church attendance would do more damage than good.
Even he knew he wasn't being fair to April by insin-
uating himself into her church. And yet, if Claymore
ruled in his favor, it would become his church as well.

"Hush, Tim. This isn't the place," the boy's father
told him.

"But Miss April helped me when I tipped over Mr.
Claymore's apples. We need to help her now." The
boy continued to glare at Will.

"Later," his father replied.

Then Pastor Johnson said, "Please be seated," and
the boy complied as Will watched elbows being
bumped and several pairs of eyes look his way. Pastor
Johnson's was among them. Everyone's in fact, except
April and her sisters. He couldn't see them from his
vantage. He hoped they couldn't see him.

The pastor cleared his throat, regaining the parishioners' attention. "Turn with me once again to Exodus, please," he said.

Will settled himself into the pew seat and opened his Bible. It had been a while since he'd done so. But he'd already given his thanks to the Almighty for providing him with Justus Wilde's land. Now he focused on the Pastor's review from last week and continuation.

"We learned how God, after giving Pharaoh so many chances, forced Pharaoh to release the Israelites from captivity. And we saw how they were led to the Red Sea. Then, with Pharaoh's army behind them and the water before them, they thought God had led them to a dead end.

"But had God deserted the Israelites? Or was it their lack of faith that caused them to raise their fists in anger to the very God who had set them free?

"As we know, God had a specific plan in mind for His people. This plan was for our benefit, too, so many years later. Because we can see step by step how God led His people from slavery. Ask yourself if you're in slavery today because you're not opening your heart to what God's plan is for your life.

"Ask yourself if you feel like you're at a dead end. Or do you have faith God will lead you from your despair?"

He went on to read several verses of the second book of the Bible, ending with the retelling of how God parted the Red Sea so His people would be free at last. He concluded by lifting his voice to lead the congregation in another song and prayer before the flock began to disperse.

Will sat in his seat for awhile, digesting the pastor's words, taking them to heart and trying to learn from them. In a way he felt like God was speaking directly to him through the pastor. God had certainly led him to the promised land. Now he just had to walk through the parted waters and he'd be home free.

"Well, I'll be," Will heard from a male voice he was familiar with from the saloon. "Staking another claim, huh, Caulder?"

He took the man's outstretched hand and shrugged. "Just felt like attending service, Ned," he replied. "Nothing wrong with that."

"Nothin' a'tall," Ned replied with a grin, until a woman behind him slapped him on the shoulder. His grin faded. "Just talking to the man, Velma darlin'."

"He's a thief in the Lord's house," Velma told him with a cold stare at Will. She ushered her husband down the aisle, leaving Will alone again.

Velma's scorn was how he should have been treated all along, Will told himself. His faith in people was actually beginning to be restored. They needed to stand up for April.

He continued to search for her, and Edwin Talbot, knowing they would most likely be together with May and June. What his gaze found instead was April and Cirrus Claymore near the far door.

Intrigued, Will watched as Claymore said something before he fingered the ribbon of April's bonnet. She pulled away and gave him a reply, which made Claymore's smile abruptly fade. Then he cocked his head to one side and the smile reappeared. He spoke again, and reached for her ribbon again. This time April didn't pull back. Even from the distance that separated them Will could see her face pale. Then she suddenly turned and fled out the door.

An intense fury surged through Will's frame as he watched Claymore smile smugly at her retreating back. He took a step toward the attorney, then remembered he was in a house of God.

Deciding to deal with Claymore later, he made his way to the door April had fled through. A bright sun greeted him as he stepped outside onto a wooden platform with a set of stairs leading to the ground. Tall pine trees lined each side of the deck. At the bottom of the stairs sprawled a grassy area where several church members stood in idle chatter. Will scanned the area, but failed to see April. He started down the stairs when a woman's voice from behind the pines stopped him.

"And then she said April was going to lure that Caulder man into marrying her just so she could stay on the farm."

"Well, I heard from Yolanda just yesterday, who heard it from Sadie, that she practically forced her attentions on him," came another female voice.

Will fisted his hands.

"You don't say? She's always been a bit forward. I'm not surprised."

He heard a sob then, coming from the pines on his other side. Sick at heart, he watched April hurry from her hiding place and around the back of the church.

Confound it!

"Did you hear something, Bea?" said the first woman.

"Hear what?"

"Oh, nothing. Well, I'd better go round up Charlie and get on home."

"Me too, Ellie."

The two women moved out of the shadows. Will didn't hesitate to finish his descent and stop in front of them. "I wouldn't believe everything I hear, ladies," he scolded. "And I certainly wouldn't repeat false rumors. Or doesn't it say something about gossiping in the Good Book?" With that he tipped his hat and left them, mouths agape, as he followed in April's wake. But she was gone.

She had a throbbing headache. She used the truth to bow out of staying at the church after Edwin agreed to see May and June home once they'd eaten their picnic lunch.

Now she led Samson toward the farm with a heavy heart. First Will had come along, and now rumors were spreading that she was trying to lure him into marriage. All that was bad enough, intolerable enough, but Cirrus's little escapade after church was her real undoing. Her worst fear had been realized when he'd told her he would recommend that his father rule in Will's favor if she didn't accept his courtship. He'd promised to tell the judge that he felt the law was on Caulder's side.

"You'll never find another man in this town, April, my mother's seen to that. She's done so for your own good. I'm perfect for you. We've always known so."

April had hurried away from him before responding, but she knew he was convinced she was going to accept his suit.

He was dead wrong though. As were Sadie and all the rest who thought April would do *anything* to keep her land. Marrying the debauched attorney was where she drew the line. And trying to manipulate Will into marriage was just as preposterous. The only thing he wanted was her land.

Which was why her head was pounding. If Cirrus went to his father, the judge was bound to rule in Will's favor.

Maybe it was for the best. Her feet were blistered from walking in the desert, just like the Israelites. She had to stop pretending her Red Sea was ever going to be parted. May would marry Edwin, and perhaps June could live with them in town. Neither girl was disliked like she was. Perhaps the best thing for April was to leave Colorado altogether. Weather permitting she could return to the east, meet her parents' families. Or perhaps she should go to California or Oregon. She had nothing to lose, and as long as her sisters were safe. . . .

She sighed and rubbed her temple before pulling Samson and the buckboard to a stop in front of the barn. She maneuvered herself down and was beginning to unharness him when she heard horse's hooves pounding into the yard.

Will was on Tate and despite her best efforts not to allow it, her heart bounded, came to a crashing halt, then began to race. Anticipation danced through her as he quickly halted and slid from the horse's back. He smacked Tate's rump and sent him off toward the paddock. Then he turned his attention to April.

"Wh-what's wrong?" she asked. He was obviously troubled. His blue eyes were darker, his brow forming a sharp V. He removed his hat and raked his hand through his wayward hair, just missing the all-but-healed cut above his eye, and leaving his locks more ruffled than matted, more ruggedly disheveled than gentlemanly sleek. One fell over his brow, making April gulp.

"Did something happen?" she questioned again when he failed to reply. "Something I should know about?"

"Something." Will repeated the word, his voice low and raw. He strode toward her with long strides, stopping inches in front of her. He sent his hat sailing onto the porch. "Yeah, you might say something happened," he added. And before she knew his intent, before she could resist him, Will grabbed her around the waist, pulled her against him, and planted his mouth on hers.

April struggled for the briefest moment before she decided kissing Will back was exactly what she wanted to do. She couldn't have fought against the thrill of his taste had she a legion of angels to help her. With a faint sigh she surrendered, molded her mouth to his and wrapped her arms around his neck.

She forgot about his treachery, forgot about her bleak future, the struggle it would take to start over—all because of him. Instead she let herself believe, just for a moment, that she was safe at last, home at last, in Will's loving arms.

A moment though, was all it lasted. Her fantasy crumbled the second Will pulled his lips from hers. The second she opened her eyes and saw him staring down at her with a tortured gaze that made the warmth flowing through her body sputter and turn to ice.

Will pressed his forehead to hers. "I never meant to hurt you," he whispered.

April wrenched herself from his embrace.

"April?"

She shook her head, felt the tears pooling in the corners of her eyes. But she wasn't about to give him the pleasure of seeing her cry. Of thinking, even for one moment that he affected her. "Who are you to think you could hurt me?" she tossed back. "If you think that anything you do will cause me pain, you're wrong. You can train every last mustang in the range and I won't care. If the judge rules in your favor, I'll leave. And gladly. You can have every decaying bit of this place."

She blinked rapidly and took a steadying breath. "You could never hurt me, Will Caulder, and I don't need your pity," she added before lifting her skirts and marching into the house.

Will chopped more wood than was necessary after he'd finished unharnessing Samson, and gave the horse, and Tate, a good rubdown and extra oats. He did so just as much to occupy his time, his own mind, as for the horses' benefit. He was still tasting the sweetness of April's lips, still feeling April in his arms—and wanting her back there.

All the while his gaze kept wandering to the front door, the window, hoping for a glimpse of her, hoping she'd come outside so he would know she was all right.

Several times he'd considered knocking on the door, demanding she open it. But then what would he do? Kiss her again? Say that he was sorry again? Sorry for what; for wanting her, or for trying to take her land away? She had made it plain she didn't want to hear his empty words. What she wanted instead was for him to forfeit his claim.

He dropped the ax with disgust and gathered an armful of wood, then headed for the woodbin, trying to make sense of all that was happening. So far he wasn't making much progress. But then why had everything added up until the moment he arrived at the farm? His fateful journey to Cripple Creek, the card game, the wager? Hindsight had made them all seem as if they'd happened just as they should have.

At April's expense?

That was where his thinking had faltered.

He lifted the trap door and let the wood fall into the bin on the porch. He was heading back for another armload when he heard carriage wheels. Edwin Talbot was driving his rig into the yard. In it sat May and June and Cirrus Claymore.

Will wondered how much worse the day could get. He kept heading for the woodpile, knowing he was in no mood to deal with the attorney yet. If pressed, he'd probably lay the man out. It was best if he just ignored Claymore and the others.

"I thought Sheriff Moss restricted you to working in the barn, Caulder," Claymore called out to ruin Will's effort.

His jaw tightened. From the corner of his eye he watched Claymore exit the buggy and assist June out. Edwin assisted May.

"Mr. Caulder has been very helpful since he arrived," June said naively. "He does a lot of chores around here."

"Does he?" Cirrus queried. "How convenient."

"There's no reason why I can't work on property that will soon be mine." Will picked up a few more logs.

"I wouldn't be too sure about that if I were you, Caulder." Cirrus sneered at Will with contempt. "Things change, you know? Something could come up at any time." He drew out the last word.

Will stopped to address him. "Like what, Claymore? My claim's pretty simple. Wilde lost, I won."

"You haven't proved it yet," Cirrus replied. "And if I have my way, I can almost guarantee you won't."

Will narrowed his gaze. "What are you alluding to, Claymore?"

"Yes, what *are* you alluding to, Mr. Claymore?" April repeated.

Will turned with the others to see her clinging to the porch rail as if it were the only thing holding her up. He tossed the wood in his arms toward the woodbin and walked to the bottom of the porch, putting himself between April and the others.

"You, you know what I mean, April," Claymore blustered. "We discussed this."

"Miss Wilde to you, Mr. Claymore," she told him. "And, no, I don't know what you mean. If you're referring to this morning's little announcement, let me remind you I never answered."

"Of course I'm referring to this morning's er . . . discussion," he bellowed. "You know that very well. And you'll stop this nonsense right now, *April*. I'm growing weary of your rebellion."

"You overstep yourself, Cirrus," she told him. "I never agreed to the terms of your proposal. And . . ." She took a steadying breath. "I never will."

"What proposal?" Will didn't have a right to ask, but that wasn't going to stop him. "What did he say to you?"

April glanced his way before returning her glare to the attorney. "He told me he was going to recommend to Judge Claymore that he rule in your favor." Her tone declared her defeat. "*If* I didn't agree to his courtship. If I did, he assured me he could get someone—a fake witness—to lie to the judge. To say that our father was coerced by you."

"April, that's quite enough!"

"Shut up, Claymore," Will spat back.

"He assumed I was desperate enough to agree to such a distasteful bargain."

"That's what you said to her in church this morning?" Will's voice shook with rage. "That's what you said to make her run out?"

"You saw me? At service this morning?" April took a step forward. "You were there?"

"Yes, I . . . yes. I saw Claymore addressing you. I

saw you slap his hand away, and run. And I heard the two women. Heard what you heard. After you ran again I set them straight."

She paled and Will would have given anything to put his arms around her, comfort her. "And you followed me back here?" she whispered.

"I did."

"Another convenience," Cirrus drawled. "As if she didn't set everything up so you'd follow. No wonder you don't need my help. The rumors must be true."

"What rumors?" June asked.

"I admit, May, I've been quite concerned." Edwin twirled his bowler in his hands. "That's why I wanted to drive you home today. And why I accepted Cirrus's request to come along. We wanted to see for ourselves what was going on out here."

"What rumors?" June cried again.

"The rumors about me trying to lure Mr. Caulder into marriage," April explained. "So I can keep the farm."

"That's what the two women were gossiping about this morning." Will stepped closer to Cirrus. "You knew about the talk and did nothing to protect your client?"

"I was trying to verify if the rumors were true," he snorted. "Sheriff Moss thought so, after he found you *inside* the house, sitting in the rocker."

"Mr. Caulder was hurt!" June exclaimed. "He had a cut on his head. Oh, this is awful." She gasped and ran up the steps to hug April.

Will felt his stomach churn.

"You knew about these rumors, Edwin? And you didn't tell me?" May whispered.

"Sheriff Moss said he found Caulder in the house, May. Sitting in the rocker as if he owned the place,"

Edwin defended. "What was I supposed to say about that?"

She lowered her gaze to the ground.

"April—"

Will planted his feet and rubbed his jaw. "I believe the lady told you not to call her by her given name, Claymore. Several times. And I think we've all heard more from you than any of us care to. Talbot, I suggest you take your friend here and head out."

"Don't try to tell me what to do," Cirrus sputtered.

"I might not own this land yet, Claymore." Will was finding it harder and harder to control himself. "But it's either mine or Miss Wilde's and I'm of the opinion she wants you gone as much as I do. You've got five seconds to get in that buggy. One—"

"This is outrageous," Cirrus spat. He looked at April. "Aren't you going to do something?"

"I can get the rifle for Mr. Caulder." She crossed her arms.

"Two."

With a huff, Cirrus entered the buggy. "Let's go, Talbot. We've seen enough."

"Enough to know that the rumors *aren't* true," Will reiterated. "Remember that. And if I hear anything to the contrary, I'll be looking for you, Claymore."

He waited for Talbot to enter the rig and turn it back toward town. When the last of the noise it created faded away, the quiet of the afternoon settled around the farm. Will had his back to the porch where the three girls stood just as silent as he was. For the life of him, he couldn't turn around. Couldn't face them. Instead, he took one step, and then another, toward the barn. It was his fault their reputations were suffering. His fault Claymore was trying to coerce April into an unwanted relationship with him. He'd done more than enough damage.

Chapter Nine

April was still feeling the effects of Will's kiss long
after Cirrus had left with Edwin, taking his disgusting
offer and innuendo with him. Long after May and June
had settled down enough to go to bed. Long after Will
had taken Tate and the mustang and ridden out.

She was bundled against the cold, sitting on the top
porch step that had been occupied by Will so fre-
quently of late. Now she doubted he'd ever sit there
again. At least for her to see. Before Judge Claymore's
ruling against her.

She told herself she was glad he'd gone. It was
probably best that she never see him again. They had
the strangest relationship; one minute they were adversaries, fighting over the same property, the next
they were allies. Well, as close to allies as April knew
how to be.

And then there was the attraction between them.

The attraction she couldn't deny any longer. Her lips still burned where he had touched her with his own. Claimed her really, his mouth insistent, demanding, possessive. She tingled when she relived the moment he had approached her in the yard earlier that day, his blue eyes molten, his jaw set. What had sparked his approach had been a mystery until he'd admitted being at church; Will had actually defended her. He'd stood up for her with Cirrus. No one had ever done that before.

And then he'd hurried back to the farm to make sure she was all right. To make her all right with his mouth and his arms around her, pulling her against the long, warm length of him.

April shivered, but the frigid night air had nothing to do with her reason why. Will had everything to do with it. And she'd lied. Told him nothing he did affected her.

She'd never let him know otherwise, and whatever *had* happened between them wouldn't happen again. She'd bury the memory, take it out once in awhile, and that was all. Soon the farm would be his. She had talked to June and May after supper. Once Judge Claymore granted Will his claim, they were going to move on. May had decided that if Edwin truly loved her, he'd try to stop her. And if not, well, they had all promised each other they'd find true love elsewhere. April knew her promise to her sisters had been empty. She knew she'd never find a man as like Will as she needed him to be, and yet one as different from him where it mattered. Will was as close to a decent man as she had ever met. But he was still a thief. And in her experience, the complete package didn't exist.

Still, she could dream, and remember, and yearn for another moment in Will's arms. Another moment when his lips were molded to hers, when her body was singing, and her blood was flowing.

She sighed and sipped her cooling coffee, while the huge Colorado sky glistened with stars all around her. Her mountains were out there too, unseen now, in the dark. And so was Will. Somewhere.

Had he gone to town? Made camp beside the river? Decided to track the mustang herd and use the rust as bait? Was he watching the same night sky that she was? Thinking about today? Their kiss? Or had he completely put it—and her—out of his mind?

She wished she could put him out of her mind. But even now she could see him staring down at her with that smoldering gaze, his hair tangled, his mouth slightly parted.

"You should be in bed."

She jumped, her coffee sloshing. She hadn't heard him return, but there he stood, holding Tate's reins in one hand, the mustang's in the other—and looking just like she thought he should.

"Sorry," he added. "I didn't mean to startle you."

April swallowed the fear in her throat and took a deep breath to settle her pounding heart. "I didn't think you'd be back," she told him.

"I didn't think so either." He sounded as weary as the horses looked.

He urged both animals into the paddock and shut the gate, then turned to face her. She could see his outline in the darkness; tall frame, broad shoulders, chiseled jaw. He stayed where he was, feet away from her, staring at her like he had earlier, just before he kissed her.

"When did your father leave this place?" he suddenly asked. "How old were you?"

She thought about telling him it was none of his

business. She'd done so before. But now it didn't seem to matter if he knew. Now it was almost as if he'd earned the privilege to ask. "I was ten when he left the last time. He'd come and gone before. He finally never came back."

"And when your mother died? How old?"

"Twelve. She finally gave up waiting for him."

Will stepped closer, stopped, then walked over and sat down beside her. Their legs brushed before he jerked his knee away. "Justus told me he was from New England."

"He was, originally." April immediately felt the warmth his closeness brought. "A shipbuilder's son with a wandering spirit, my mother told me. He talked her into heading west. I was born in Kentucky, May, Missouri, and June in Kansas. All along the way. He kept promising my mother they'd plant roots when they reached the next town, the next bend, the next river. She put her foot down when they reached this place. But it didn't keep him home. At first he left on short trips, just to see what was out there, he'd tell her. He always brought back a cinnamon stick for each of us, and stories of his adventures.

"He'd stay around for a little while, then get restless again and make up some excuse to head out. Each trip got longer."

April paused. She had never talked about her father before. When May and June brought him up, she'd tell them to forget him, that he wasn't worth their thoughts. "The girls would plague my mother, wanting to know when he was coming back, just so they could have a cinnamon stick and watch his eyes light up as he told us another story. So my mother began making us cinnamon bread once a week, and creating stories of her own. Stories that . . ."

"Stories that . . . ?"

April shrugged. "You don't want to hear all this."

He didn't answer. Instead she suddenly felt his knee again. Pressing against her own, staying there. Her pulse sped up.

"My father inherited our land from his father, who settled it with his father after they left Germany," Will said. "My grandfather was a baron. He and my grandmother had twelve children."

April could barely nod. She was more interested in Will's knee against hers than his words.

"The land was everything to my family." He pulled at a piece of calloused skin on his thumb. "We respected it, cherished it. We had a good life because of it. I spent my childhood fishing, running through the woods, and learning everything I could from my father and grandfather. They were good men."

"Were?" April turned to look at him. "Are they both gone then?"

Will shook his head. "My father is still alive, but failing. The war devastated him."

"And you?" she whispered. "Did the war devastate you, too?"

He glanced at her from the corner of his eye, then slowly turned his head until he was looking at her directly. "And me, in a way, yes," he replied. "The war took its toll on all of us. I was a Lieutenant for the Blue and Gray. But the Union troops didn't know that when they came to burn our plantation. And they wouldn't listen to my father's explanation, or my mother's pleas. Or . . . my sister's screams. We lost everything at the hands of our own. And I wasn't there to stop it."

April looked at him, saw the regret in his eyes. Regret that made him feel like he had let them down. "It wasn't your fault," she told him.

He shrugged. "I wish I felt the same way."

"I . . ." She glanced down at her cup of cold coffee. "I guess I'm grateful my sisters and I were here, removed from all of that."

She felt Will's finger touch the bottom of her chin, stealing her breath. He added just enough pressure to turn her head back to face him. When she looked into his eyes she saw remorse, pain churning there.

"So am I," he whispered, before he pulled her closer still with just the tug of his finger. Pulled her toward him as he leaned toward her.

When their lips touched it was as if the sheerest fabric had touched her; the kiss of the sun, a flower's blossom. April closed her eyes, savoring the feel.

"April?" Will's warm breath teased her cheek. "I'm going to kiss you again. All right?"

"Yes," she breathed back. *Oh, yes.*

But when she heard the horses blow and snort, her eyes opened. Will looked toward the paddock expectantly, only to listen to the quiet as the horses settled again.

She heard him exhale. "They're as tired as I am." His voice was weary. "As tired as you must be."

"I can't sleep."

"Not surprisingly." He stood up then, taking her with him. His hands were on her arms. He moved one hand to the tender skin beneath her eye, caressing it with his thumb. "Try."

"Will?" she said then, taking hold of his hand to stop him from leaving. "What was he like before he died? My father?" She had no idea where the question came from. She had no idea why she wanted to know.

But she kept Will's hand covered in hers, waiting, as she saw him begin to contemplate her words.

"I only saw him drunk. Twice, a week apart. He was like any other drunk; his words were slurred, his head kept drooping. But once in a while, it seemed to me there was an awareness in him. He kept eyeing me as if he was trying to learn something. And he had questions, too. He wanted to know who I was, where I'd come from, where I was going. He was sharp, a contrast. And . . ."

"Yes?"

"He kept saying to Lyonel Sims something about finding the right one."

"I see," she said. But she didn't. She dropped her hand. "Cirrus—"

"Shhh," Will told her.

"But you defended me and I—"

"Claymore is a fool. If you ever did consider his proposal I'd be the first to protest."

She smiled at that and lowered her head once more, only to have Will lift it. When she looked at him again his eyes were as intense as she had ever seen them.

"You are the most beautiful woman I have ever seen," he whispered. "I've waited to see your smile." And then he did kiss her.

April heard her own small moan as she parted her lips, fascinated by the feel of him, by her own need to respond to him. She wanted to crawl into his skin, get closer than she could by just a kiss. She wrapped her hands in his hair, tugging, pressing herself closer against the bulk of overcoats and wool.

When he broke the kiss the cold air shocked her where his lips had been.

"Tell me about Cirrus. Why won't he leave you alone? What happened between you and his mother?"

Her thoughts wandered back reluctantly. "It wasn't his mother—at first—who was the problem. You see, after my mother died, Judge Claymore came to help us bury her and then he said his wife would come by to see if we needed any help. But she sent Cirrus instead. And he made it clear he wanted something in return for the foodbasket he had from her. He tried to kiss me."

"But you were only twelve."

She nodded. "I pushed him away, frightened, and told him never to come back. I don't know exactly what he told his mother but I know enough. He must have told her I refused their help. But at the same time, his attraction never faded. I think it's only because he can't have what he wants. But he's been pursuing me ever since."

Will exhaled roughly. "May told me you'd always planned on raising horses here. After she and June married."

She nodded again.

"You had your eye on the mustangs, didn't you?"

She shrugged. "It wasn't important."

His hand smoothed her hair. "Dreams are always important. Go inside, April," he urged. "Tomorrow will be a better day."

April slowly turned away from him. She didn't want to. And she wanted to tell him so. But she knew he was right. She needed sleep and so did he. She just wasn't sure today had been such a bad day after all.

He couldn't have slept in the barn if it was the last shelter around. A cold night under the stars was what he needed. What he got—after he'd made sure April had gone inside.

He used the cold to keep him awake, keep him

thinking—praying. All this time he'd been so sure Justus Wilde had been put in his path in order to provide him a home for his family. That he was being rewarded for his dedication and commitment to his family. During the journey he'd made from high in the mountains of Cripple Creek to the flatlands his certainty had increased.

And then he'd met April.

He'd soon questioned why he'd been granted reprieve at her expense. At first he'd rationalized, telling himself he couldn't second-guess the situation. That perhaps his arrival was the push April needed toward something new and better—away from the farm.

No longer.

He was now more certain than ever that April's place was on the farm. So where was his?

From his place outside the barn door where he sat with a heavy wool blanket around his shoulders he lifted his eyes to heaven. *I wasn't imagining anything. My path was made clear. I was supposed to come here. Justus Wilde didn't have to wager this land. I wanted him to back out. So now what?*

Silence greeted him. Silence, and yet a soft peace. With a deflated sigh, he glanced toward the cabin and noticed the smoke beginning to curl from the chimney. The girls were up. The Wilde girls. Wild flowers. Beautiful, stunning wildflowers. Living their entire lives with only the bare essentials, and yet happy to be together.

In contrast, his family had been traumatized by a four-year war. And were floundering instead of rebounding.

He was glad he had been here to defend April yesterday. Glad Claymore had been put in his place. And for the first time Will wondered if perhaps that was the reason he'd been sent to the farm. It could have nothing to do with the land and everything to do with protecting April Wilde. And he'd trade the land for her in a heartbeat.

Will stood up, the blanket falling. *He'd trade the land? In a heartbeat? For April?*

Staring at the cabin once more, he reached down and grabbed the blanket. He strode into the barn, tossed the blanket over Tate's stall where the black was standing. "We're going for a ride, boy," he told the horse who eyed him. "And don't give me one of your looks. You got more rest than I did."

It didn't take Will long to track down Judge Claymore. He was seated with his wife at a table on the back veranda of their well-appointed home. The butler had announced Will's unexpected visit while Will waited at the front door. Then, with his employer's permission the butler had escorted Will through the formal living area, through a set of French doors with glass panes, and onto the whitewashed veranda.

Sadie Claymore set down the stemmed glass she was holding and smiled haughtily when she saw him. She was a plump matron. She reminded Will of a Swedish boarding house owner he'd met in St. Louis, known for her scorn. It was odd to see the woman wearing anything other than a frown.

"Mr. Caulder, how pleasant it is to see you."

Will tipped his head her way. "I apologize for interrupting your breakfast."

"Not at all. I'm sure you must have good news if you've gone this length. Did Sheriff Moss find your second witness?"

Judge Claymore continued to cut his steak into small pieces, popping one into his mouth and chewing.

The small round table where he sat was laden with a full accoutrement of food items and tableware. A maid approached to refill his coffee cup.

"Not exactly," Will answered Mrs. Claymore.

"Then what can I do for you, my boy?" the judge said after swallowing.

He had proved he was a no-nonsense man. He was blunt as well. Will couldn't say that he didn't like that in the man. And since he didn't want to play games either, he figured Claymore would respect his decision to come right to the point. He only wished the judge's wife would leave first. But since the woman was making no movement to do so, Will pushed on. "I'd like to withdraw my claim on the Wilde land. I've reconsidered."

"What?" Mrs. Claymore protested. She rose from her seat, aghast. "That's impossible."

"Why is that?" Will kept his eye on the judge.

Claymore finished chewing and swallowing another biteful of ham. Then he set his fork and knife beside his plate, wiped his face with his linen napkin and appraised Will. "Strange request seein's how you were all fired up about the place."

"I realize that, judge. But certain things have changed my mind."

"You bein' threatened?" Claymore asked.

"No. Of course not." Will was surprised by the question.

"Coerced?"

"No. Nothing like that. What do I have to do to formally end my claim on the land?"

"You must be in love then," the judge replied.

Will stared at the man as if he'd been caught.

"Oh, please," Mrs. Claymore piped in. "Which of those three strumpets would attract a southern gentleman? No, that can't possibly be the reason. Have you just realized what an awful place the Wilde farm is and that you're better off without it?"

Will felt his insides begin to seethe. "I can assure you, Mrs. Claymore, the Wilde sisters are no strumpets. They're hard-working, respectable young ladies who have overcome a great deal in their lives. Including you. And your son—who happens to want one of those girls you call strumpets. April is much too good for him, and was just a young girl when he lied to you about her, telling you she didn't want your help when in fact she just didn't appreciate him trying to kiss her. Don't you think she's suffered enough? I do. And I'm going to start telling people so." He knew he had just shot himself in the foot. He expected Claymore to boot him from the property. Instead, the judge smiled behind his napkin.

"Always did like those three young ladies. Had a lot of gumption they did. Don't know where I went wrong with that boy of mine."

Mrs. Claymore tossed her napkin on the table. She glared at her husband for a full ten seconds before she turned that glare on Will and spun on her heel to disappear.

"Now then." The judge cleared his throat. "I'm going to pay for this, Caulder. So your reason better be a good one."

Chapter Ten

April was returning from a visit to her mother's grave when the commotion caught her attention. She slowed her pace and sighted several people standing in the yard. May and June were among the group of two men and two women. They all appeared to be in a state of agitation.

April hurried down the embankment, catching words as she went.

"Can't be!"

"A long way."

"Tired."

"Will Caulder."

She practically froze when she heard Will's name and studied the profiles of the strangers more closely.

"April!" she heard then as June squealed her name. Her sister ran up the slope to her. "There's a family here. Mr. Caulder's family. His mother, father, sister,

143

and a cousin who decided to come along. His mother says Will sent for them and they're going to *live* here."

April had known they were on their way. He'd told her as much. But knowing so and seeing them were two different things. And he wasn't here to greet them. He'd left early again. This time leaving the mustang behind. He'd be back, but when? And what was she supposed to do with his family until his return?

She continued down the hill, June in tow, wondering when this nightmare was going to end. And Will had promised her today would be a better day.

"Good afternoon," she greeted with a weak smile. "I'm April Wilde. You've met my sisters, May and June. You must be Mr. and Mrs. Caulder, Abigail and . . ."

"Reynold Duncan," the eldest woman offered. "My nephew from Tennessee." She was tall and trim, her grass-green day dress simple but fashionably made of worsted wool. She had on a matching silk hat that was pinned neatly into her uplifted and coiled graying dark hair and she carried a matching parasol. April put her age somewhere around sixty years. She also noted the woman had kind, but perplexed eyes. They were the exact cobalt color of her son's.

"Good afternoon," Mr. Duncan said with a sweeping bow that made June giggle. He was young, handsome, well-appointed in his gray suit and shining black shoes, and couldn't have been more than twenty. "Will doesn't know I came along. Is he about? We want to surprise him."

"Or have we made a mistake?" the older man asked, clothed similarly to Duncan. "We had reason to believe this was his property. Perhaps we read the directions wrong. These two young ladies here, your sisters did you say, are as confused as we are." He looked much older than his wife, his features worn, his eyes droopy. His hair was thinning and completely silver.

April tried to hold her smile. She didn't want to be the one to tell Will's family about their tug-of-war. That was his responsibility. "You have the right place," she replied. "We know your son, yes. He's just not here right now."

"Oh, dear." Mrs. Caulder touched her gloved hand to her lips. "I was so looking forward to seeing him. Do you know when to expect him?"

"It's been ages since we've seen him," Abigail put in. She too was dressed in the latest eastern fashion, her overskirt a pretty lavender and cream lace to match her bodice and jacket.

April kept her smile. She felt sorry for the travelers. "I can't say when he'll return. I'm not sure where he went."

"We should leave then," Mr. Caulder replied. "Come back later. We didn't know there were three . . . ah . . . ladies . . . that is, is this his property?"

"Papa!" Abigail interrupted before April could reply. "We've been traveling forever. I don't want to go anywhere else. And Will could return at any time."

"Yes, dear, but, we don't want to disturb these young women any longer."

"Is this our son's property?" Mrs. Caulder put in.

April sighed silently. What was she supposed to tell these weary people? That their son was trying to steal her land? That a judge was going to determine who owned it?

"Something is wrong, my dear?" Mr. Caulder added.

April's heart broke. He seemed like such a nice man. After talking to Will she knew he cared for his father deeply. Why couldn't her father have been so wonderful?

She glanced down the road, hoping to see Will returning from wherever he was. "I'm sure your son will explain as soon as he returns. Until then you're welcome to come into the house and wait for him."

"Thank goodness!" exclaimed Will's sister. The woman was an attractive younger version of her mother. She strode forward and extended her hand. "I'm Abigail Caulder." She shook April's hand before moving on to May. "I think I'd die if I had to get back in that buggy. Between the train and the buggy and the dust . . . well, I'm sure you understand."

"Please follow me." April extended her hand toward the house, glancing down the road again, hoping to see Will. She'd never entertained guests before and had little in the way of refreshments. And she knew Will's family would find the interior of the house lacking. She felt drab next to them in her faded brown.

But Mrs. Caulder graciously smiled as April stood aside for them to enter. She motioned her to the worn sofa while June and Abigail began to chatter like old friends.

"Ah, this is quite the thing," Mr. Duncan sighed comfortably as he seated himself on the sofa. "Much needed, isn't it uncle?"

"I'll bring out a tray of jam and biscuits," May whispered in April's ear.

April nodded her thanks and folded her hands, hoping Will would hurry back.

April rose from the rocker an hour later when she heard Will's greeting outside the house. The rest of his family went quiet.

"Will!" Abigail finally cried out, rising from the

straight-backed chair May had pulled into the living area for her. She had been having a lively conversation with June. The two girls had become instant friends. "Mother, he's here!"

"My son!" Mrs. Caulder breathed. She clasped her hands and blinked rapidly. "Please understand," she apologized. "It's been two years since we've seen him."

April didn't need any explanations. In the past several minutes she'd learned Will's family thought the world of him. Every glowing term had been connected with his name.

They all stood now, making a dash for the door. April, May, and June stood aside as the door opened from outside and Will stood at the threshold.

There was silence as they stared at one another. Then he smiled and began to chuckle. "I wasn't expecting you for another several days. How'd you get here?"

His mother sniffed and flung her arms wide, embracing him. Abigail followed, sobbing openly. Mr. Caulder hung back, but even he sniffed and rubbed his nose. And Mr. Duncan patted Will loudly on the back.

"Uncle Henry gave us passage for the train, dear," Mrs. Caulder explained when she'd completed her hug.

April had already heard the story.

"I'm so grateful we didn't have to take a stagecoach, although we so appreciate the funds you send for that purpose." Abigail picked up where her mother left off. "We had our own private car."

"Father knows the owner," Reynold added. "Much better way to travel."

Will's smile widened. "And what brings you west,

cousin?" he greeted Reynold. "I never thought you'd leave Tennessee."

"Decided to see a bit of the world," Reynold replied, grabbing the lapels of his coat. "Glad I did, too."

"We hired the buggy in Denver," Abigail went on. "Is that the largest town here? I didn't see an opera house or—"

"Never mind all that now, Abigail," her mother scolded. "Let me have a look at you, son."

The tight lines April had noticed around Will's eyes faded as he allowed his mother her perusal. There was no doubt he was relieved by the safe arrival of his family. April couldn't blame him. She had already begun to like them and now understood why he'd wanted to help them so much.

"April?"

She startled when Will called her name. A wariness was reflected in his eyes as he moved to her side.

"I see you've all met?"

He was really asking her if things were all right. If she was angry by the early arrival of his family, if she had taken her anger out on them, offended them. For a moment she thought about teasing him just to see him squirm, but when he looked at her with eyes bright with questions, she took pity on him. "You have a very nice family," she told him.

"And these three lovely girls have been most hospitable," Mr. Caulder intoned. "But son, is there something we should know about? Miss Wilde said you'd explain."

Will kept his gaze on April. *You didn't tell them*, it said. *You could have, but you didn't.* "I'll be back in just a few minutes," he told her. "I need to talk to you, too. But first I've got to talk to my family." He turned back to them. "Let's go outside. I'll clarify."

April stared at the closed door, mixed with emotion. She was happy Will and his family had been reunited. Sad because she'd never enjoy the same thing. Mostly she was frightened to know the Caulders had come to join their son and renew their dreams.

At the expense of her own.

"I wish we had a family like that," June whispered.

"We had the best mother in the world," May replied. "She's just not here anymore."

"I know." June rubbed her eyes. "I just mean now. Abigail's very lucky."

April smiled. "But she doesn't have two wonderful sisters."

Chapter Eleven

The day of the hearing April left the sanctuary of the cabin with the water pail in hand, knowing there would be no further delays. Today her future would be decided. It was an oddly comforting notion. She was tired of the wait, tired of the heart-spinning wonder. At least after today she'd know whether she was staying or leaving.

She headed down the porch steps for the river, stopping up short when she saw Will leading Tate from the barn. When he saw her, he tipped his hat, smiled, and began to brush Tate.

April felt her heart tear. They hadn't talked since his family's arrival three days before. He'd returned to thank her for providing them hospitality, but he'd been busy with them in Denver ever since, where they were staying at the hotel until Judge Claymore offered his ruling.

Their talk had been short, and paled in comparison to the day prior, when he'd defended her against Cirrus. The day she'd kissed him—and kissed him some more.

The day she'd admitted to herself that she loved him.

She sighed now, still fighting what she knew to be true. And wondering if all the women in her family were doomed to fall for the wrong man. Her mother had. Now April had, too.

She didn't want to love Will. He was a black-hearted thief. He had taken advantage of her father's weakness for his own gain. And he was trying to do the same to her.

But April wasn't go to let him win so easily. She'd thought Cirrus had made good his threat to talk to his father about awarding Will the land. But as the days passed without word, she'd realized Will had put enough fear into him—or maybe there had been too many witnesses—for Cirrus to do so. But she wasn't placing any bets that he'd do much to defend her either. So she was prepared to do so herself. She would stand up in front of the entire town and state her case. And then, if Claymore still ruled against her, she'd accept his decision. She'd turn her back on the farm— her dreams—and accept her fate. Maybe the farm wasn't where she was supposed to be.

With a sigh, she pulled her gaze from Will and made her way to the river, pulled the water they needed for the morning chores, and returned to the house to find him and Tate gone. Again. Most likely he'd already left for court. For the last time.

The thought pierced April's heart like a bullet. How could he kiss her one minute and try to steal from her the next? How could he, in good conscience, ask Claymore to give him her home?

Oh, she cried. *Why hasn't there been a way to make him leave?*

She left with her sisters an hour later. She knew the moment they arrived that the courthouse was as crowded as ever. She was getting used to the attention. Used to the stares and the curiosity. So instead of parking away from the courthouse, she drove the wagon through the milling crowd, determined not to stop until she was directly in front of the building.

"Morning, Miss June," someone called as usual. "Miss May."

"Morning, Miss April," came another voice. The greeting startled her. She turned toward the voice, only to see a throng of faces. But someone *had* greeted her. And with kindness in their voice.

"We hope you win, Miss April," she heard then, much to her amazement. "Hope Judge rules in your favor."

Again she looked into the crowd where the second voice had come from, to no avail. "Am I hearing right?" she asked May and June.

"I think so," May responded. "Look, isn't that Tim Elliott?" The teen had taken Solomon's bridle. "He's steering us through the crowd."

"Out of the way!" another man shouted. "Miss April needs to get through!"

April couldn't believe what was happening. Stan Elliott had moved alongside his son and was parting the crowd. Tim brought Solomon to a stop and tied the wagon to the post.

"Mind if I help you down, Miss Wilde?"

April froze. Mr. Dortch, the owner of the mercantile, stood at the wagon, peering up at her. Pastor Johnson was beside him.

"I don't understand," she whispered.

"Been a fool," Dortch grumbled. "Should'a known not to listen to a bunch of ol' biddies."

"People can have a change of heart, April. You know that," Pastor Johnson added with a smile. "I think a few people started voicing what they've felt for a long while now. Specifically that you've been maligned long enough. Word's spread."

"But—"

"Come on down, girl. You've got a hearin' ta get to," Mr. Dortch encouraged. He held up his hand for her to take.

"Accept the offering, my dear," Pastor Johnson pleaded. "You were a child when you and Sadie clashed. You're not a child any longer."

"You're right," she said to Pastor Johnson. "I'm not a child any longer." She extended her hand to the burly German. When she was securely on the ground, she thanked him.

"Now walk into that courthouse with faith that the outcome will be exactly what the Lord wants." Pastor Johnson patted her shoulder. "You're His child and He cares for you. He isn't going to leave you in the wilderness."

April swallowed the lump in her throat and nodded, feeling stronger than she had in days. She turned toward the building, flanked by her sisters. She felt another hand patting her shoulder, and more kind words. She fought away tears and smiled.

Then she was standing at the courthouse door and Will was there, his family behind him. She had to stop. They were blocking the door. Mrs. Caulder's eyes were red. She held a handkerchief to her nose. Her husband cradled his wife in the nook of his arm and tipped his hat to April, his gaze solemn.

"Cirrus is already inside," Will said. He rubbed his brow and took a step toward her. "Will you walk in with me this time?"

She needed to tell him no. How could she walk side by side with her enemy? But with her heart in tatters, she found herself nodding. This might be the last time she'd ever be near him.

Will moved beside her and took her hand, placing it on his forearm. April felt her head spin. Too soon he deposited her at the table she had occupied twice before and moved to his own. Beside her Cirrus scowled and said nothing. And then Judge Claymore arrived. He pounded his gavel.

"Both parties are here again, I see. Now then, let's see if we can't end this thing." He rubbed his chin while scanning the papers in front of him, then cleared his throat. "We have a sworn statement from the first witness. Sheriff Moss was looking for the second." He was silent again. The air in the room was so thick April could almost taste it.

"It appears the second witness was found."

Everyone gasped until Claymore glared at them. They quickly quieted.

April clenched her hands, the confidence Pastor Johnson had only a short time ago reinstilled in her flying away. She needed a miracle. She needed God to part her Red Sea. And if He didn't, she needed a wagonload of grace to let go.

The judge shuffled through more papers. "Ah, here it is. A declaration from the second witness." He silently read through the statement. "Well now, it appears—"

"Your honor, may I address the court?"

April spun her head to Will. He was standing with his hands pressed against the table top.

"Ahem," Judge Claymore grumbled. "I don't think it's necessary that you do this, son?"

"But it is."

Claymore sank back in his leather chair. "Go on then."

Will rounded the table. "Judge, I want to withdraw my claim," he said loud enough for all to hear, and as the courtroom erupted April's heart lurched.

Judge Claymore pounded his gavel. When the assembled quieted, Will went on. "I've thought the whole thing through, and well . . ." He turned to April. "I feel I took advantage of Justus Wilde. He was drunk. I should have never allowed myself to play poker that night. And even though I gave him the chance to fold—to back out—I knew his pride would stand in the way."

April silently groaned. Could it be true? Was this the moment she had been waiting for? Were her troubles over now?

Oh, Will, do you mean it?

"So, you see." He turned back to the judge. "I don't deserve the Wilde property. I withdraw my—"

"Wait jus' a dern'd minute!"

Her heart plunging, April pivoted to see a man from the audience stand up. He was old and grizzled. He had a full gray beard and long straggly hair, and he was stooped. But he shuffled forward to the swinging doors in quick fashion.

"Name's Lyonel Sims, Judge," he said. "I'm that there second witness." He pointed. "That there document yer holdin's from me."

April closed her eyes. How much more shock could she take?

"And in it you say Justus Wilde knew what he was doing," Judge Claymore replied with a lifted brow.

"He was drunk," Will protested.

Cirrus stood. "Judge, just get on with this. Caulder's said his peace. Read the man's statement and rule."

"And why are you so all-fired to have a ruling?" the judge countered.

Cirrus bristled. "Because Miss Wilde has suffered enough and as her attorney—"

"He's no longer my attorney, Your Honor," April said, standing as well. "I don't want or need Mr. Claymore's kind of advice."

The judge lifted a thick brow.

Cirrus gaped and sputtered. "You–you can't *dismiss* me!"

"Yes she can," Will said.

"Yes she can," the judge reiterated. "Cirrus, take your things and sit in the crowd if you want to stay. I can't say as I blame her."

"But—"

"Before I tell the world what a blundering fool I think you are!"

Cirrus peered at his father, Will, then April. "We aren't through, you and me," he said, before he slammed his file closed, grabbed his briefcase and bumped into Lyonel Sims as he made his way from the courtroom.

"Now then, I want no more outbursts!" the Judge bellowed.

The room grew deathly quiet as everyone waited for his next words.

"Sims?"

"Yes, sir?"

"What are you doing here?"

"Er, I . . . that is . . ." The prospector glanced at

April and May and June. His eyes were bloodshot and weary. "I wanted to see this here happenin' for myself. After the sheriff found me, I reckoned I'd come on down the mountain for a look-see."

"But you signed your statement. Are you changing it now?"

"No sirree, sir. Justus knew what he was doin'." He shook his head. "But after hearin' this here fella, I thought I'd tell y'all the rest of the story."

"The rest of the story?" Judge Claymore probed.

April fell back into her chair, mouth agape.

"Well, er, yeah. Seein's how this fella is about to give up the land. Justus wouldn't 'ave wanted that, so's, bein' his partner and all fer longer than I can recollect, I thought I'd better step in and say so before y'all did somethin' Justus didn't want."

Judge Claymore was quiet, thoughtful. "And why did Mr. Wilde want this man—this particular man— to have his land?"

Sims scratched his beard. "Well now, Your Honor, sir, cause'n he got to know Caulder, and he liked what he saw. I can still hear 'im sayin', 'This is the one, this is the one should have my land'."

April remembered Will telling her something like that the night she had asked him about her father.

"And why did he like Mr. Caulder?"

"Cause'n he was honest."

Will took a step in Sims' direction. "But I wasn't. I took advantage of him when he was drunk."

"Says who?" Sims asked, his bloodshot eyes widening.

"Says me," Will replied. "You saw him. He couldn't have been in his right mind."

"He was never more so," Sims claimed.

Another hush fell over the room.

April could tell Will was disturbed by Sims' attempts to thwart him. She was disturbed. It was as if the man was going to make certain Will got the farm no matter what.

"Mr. Sims," Will began. "I don't want the Wilde property. Before God in heaven and all of you, I confess I took advantage of Justus Wilde's condition to obtain what I wanted.

"Except I didn't know then that Justus Wilde had three lovely daughters living on the farm. I didn't know then that I'd fall in love with his eldest daughter."

April felt the air whoosh out of her. "What?" she whispered, so low no one could hear her.

"Therefore, as I've tried to state before, I withdraw—"

"But that was the entire reason Justus wanted you to have the land," Sims interrupted and at once all eyes focused on him again.

"What are you talking about, Sims?" Claymore asked.

"I've been tryin' to make that clear, Judge." He spread his aged hands. "Look here, Justus wasn't drunk when he bet the land. He was sick."

"What?" Will and April said at the same time.

"Yes, sirree. He knew he was dyin'." He faced April, pivoting his gaze to encompass May and June. "Doc said he had lung fever. He was gonna come on back here. See his girls, he told me. But he got sicker real fast. Couldn't go. So's he decided to find someone who'd take care of you's." He nodded toward Will. "This here young fella comes along. He's smart as a whip, honest as the day he was born. Yer Pa likes him real well, so's we get him in a card game and Justus loses to him—on purpose."

"He did *what*?" Will bellowed.

April couldn't stop the tears from falling from her eyes. She knew May and June were sobbing as well. Had their father truly loved them? Had he tried, in the end, to make up for his desertion?

She swiped away the tears, determined to focus.

"Now don't go gettin' yer dander up," Sims told Will. "You was a good enough poker player. Justus was a bit better. He'd run out'a time."

"So he used me as his pawn?"

Sims shrugged. "He figured you'd come on down the mountain and take care a his daughters. It'n 'pears he was right."

"Yes, it does," Judge Claymore agreed. "It certainly does. Well, this changes everything, doesn't it? Mr. Caulder, would you like to withdraw your request that I dismiss your claim? I for one, after hearing Mr. Sims, believe Justus Wilde had every intention of doing exactly what he did. He was more than in his right mind."

"I . . ."

April gained her feet. "My father had no idea that Mr. Caulder would take care of me and my sisters. The fact is, he hasn't—" She paused to reconsider. Hadn't Will fixed everything that needed fixing? Hadn't he made sure they had enough firewood and a man's protection? But even so, he had still determined to kick them off their land—until he'd had a change of heart. Until he fell in love with—She shook her head to clear it.

"I still withdraw," Will said suddenly. He strode through the swinging doors and began to walk down the aisle toward the exit.

"Wait just a darn minute, young man!" bellowed Claymore. "You don't walk out of my court unless I

tell you so. Would you like me to find you in contempt?"

Will turned back to face the judge. "We discussed
this last week. You knew I was going to withdraw."

He did? They had? A week ago?

April crumbled into her seat again.

"I recall the conversation, Mr. Caulder," the judge
said. "But things have changed. Most definitely
changed. I'd be altering a dead man's last will and
testament if I allowed you to withdraw. Something I'm
not about to do."

"Judge," Will began to protest.

"Therefore, based on eyewitness testimony—"

"Judge, don't—"

"I rule that the Wilde property has legally been ob-
tained by Will Caulder." Claymore banged his gavel.
"This court is adjourned."

The eruption that followed was frantic. June and
May raced through the swinging doors to embrace
April. A slew of supporters tossed them words of con-
solation. More evident was the throng crowding
around Will, patting him on the back, offering him
congratulations. He didn't appear pleased at all. He
wore a scowl. His eyes kept darting to April before
someone else would draw his attention away.

April had her own concerns.

"Oh, April, what are we going to do?" cried June.

"Do you think we'll make it to Oregon before winter sets in?" asked May.

She didn't have the answers. "We'll be fine. We
knew this might happen," she told them. "We'll think
about it. Mr. Caulder isn't going to kick us off the
farm tonight. He'll give us time."

But would he? She had no idea. Had he really been
trying to withdraw his claim, or had that been a tactic

for victory? "May, you drive Solomon home. I need some time to think. Time alone." April rose on wobbly legs and glanced at the side door Claymore had disappeared through. She was going to use the same door whether he liked it or not.

She stepped back a pace, needed desperately to escape. "I'll see you both later," she said and hurried for the exit.

Will pushed his way through the mob, his thoughts on April as he tried to make his way to her and May and June. He needed to assure them, tell them he was giving them back the land. Put their fears to rest. Unfortunately with every step he took, someone was there wanting to congratulate him. And when he looked to the table April had occupied only a moment earlier, it was empty.

Anxiously scanning the room, he saw May and June talking with Edwin, but no April. He had to practically shove his way to their sides.

"Where is she?" he asked without preliminary.

May and June stared at him.

"I didn't want this to happen," he reminded them.

"She said she needed time alone to think about what we're going to do," May offered. She blinked back a tear. "She told us to go home. She said you wouldn't make us leave for a few days at least."

"I won't make you leave at all, May." Will hurried for the door, pushing his way through the remnant of the mulling crowd.

When he'd finally reached the street, his hair blowing in the breeze and the tepid sun offering him a bit of warmth, he searched up and down the boardwalk for signs of her, to no avail.

Why in the world was she being so stubborn? Hadn't she heard him declare his love for her?

He suddenly saw a flutter of pale green—the color of the skirt she was wearing. It disappeared around the corner at the end of the last building on the boardwalk.

Will jogged down the street, dodging horse riders, loaded-down wagons, strolling mothers and boys playing tag. When he reached the corner, he slowed.

"Don't tell me I didn't try to warn you," Cirrus's voice rang out to stop him in his tracks. "If you'd only listened to me. But you've always thought you were better than me, didn't you. The high and mighty Miss April Wilde. Even though everyone knew your father was a drunk and your mother a—"

Will heard the slap.

"Don't you dare slander my mother," April's voice warned. "My mother was the most special woman who ever lived."

A short silence followed before Will heard Cirrus chuckle decidedly. "Well, at least you've learned your lesson. I don't know why but I'm willing to forgive you. Why I still want you. I could have any girl in town. Just remember that when you're living off my generosity."

"Are you serious?" There was incredulity in April's voice.

"I wish I weren't. I hope you appreciate my sacrifice. Sometimes I think I'm mad for wanting you so much."

"You are mad," April told him. "Mad if you think I would ever consider you. Haven't I made myself very clear? You disgust me, Mr. Claymore. You always have."

"Don't make me angry, April," Cirrus growled. "I've put up with this long enough. No one else will have you, you know. No one else would put up with you."

"That might be so. But I'll live alone the rest of my life rather than give in to the likes of you."

"I'm sure that'll be just what happens." There was certainty in Claymore's voice. "But one day you'll come running to me. One day you'll be grateful I've rescued you. Because I'll never stop making your life miserable until you do. And you'll learn to respect me. Believe me, April."

"Miss Wilde to you." Will stepped around the corner. He had heard enough. It was all he could do not to lunge for Cirrus's throat. "When are you going to get that straight, Claymore? April has never given you permission to use any other name. In fact, she's more than tired of you addressing her in any way."

Cirrus backed up a pace. "You stay out of this, Caulder. You got what you wanted. Go build a pig pen or plow a field."

"And pass up the chance of seeing you brought to heel once and for all?" Will grinned sarcastically. "I thought perhaps your father had finally done so back there in the courthouse. You are thick-skinned. But it's time you learned two things. First, you're never to come close to Miss Wilde again. Ever. Second, you're to get this notion that she's supposed to be grateful to you out of your head. There's nothing to be grateful for except that you haven't been a bigger nuisance."

Cirrus backed up a step, clearly intimidated by Will's anger. "April," he said. "Don't let him ruin everything. Come away with me and I'll forgive you." He tried to take her by the arm. His attempt fell short when Will's knuckles connected with his jaw.

Cirrus spun around and fell to his knees.

"I'm not a violent man. But if you don't think I'm

serious about this, Claymore, think again." Will balled
fists at his sides, then released them, suddenly calm
again. "You touch Miss Wilde again—ever—and it'll
be the last time you touch anyone. Get up, Cirrus. Get
up, and start walking. And don't you ever let me hear
you even murmur a greeting to Miss Wilde. She's not
yours to talk to and she never will be."

Cirrus quickly rose to his feet, fear now in his eyes.
He touched his finger to his chin and came away with
smeared blood. Then darting one last look at April, he
stumbled away.

Will waited a brief moment before he faced April.
"I don't think he'll bother you any more."

"Thank you. Again," she whispered. "I only wish I
had some way of repaying you every time you come
to my aid, but I don't, so I'm not going to pretend I
do. I just hope this is the last time you have to inter-
vene on my behalf." He watched as she began to move
down the boardwalk. "Good day, Mr. Caulder."

"April, stop being so stubborn," Will admonished.

She paused and faced him. "Are you going to pick
up where Cirrus left off?"

"Are you going to pretend nothing happened back
there in Judge Claymore's courtroom?"

"A great deal happened as I recall. You won. I lost.
If I'm supposed to congratulate you like everyone else
did, I hate to disappoint you, but that's one thing I
can't do."

"You know that's not what I meant, or want. Why
are you doing this? I tried—"

"To withdraw your claim? Yes, I heard. A clever
trick, Mr. Caulder. I tried something like that. Turning
the tables and gaining sympathy from Judge Claymore
was perfect."

Will frowned. "April Wilde, you know very well that's not why I tried to withdraw my claim."

"Hey Caulder! Let's have a drink and celebrate!"

Will turned to see a group of men walking his way. He lifted his hand to ward them off. "Not this time. I'm a bit busy."

"Busy? Doing what?" one of the men replied.

When Will turned back to face April, he understood the question. She had disappeared once again.

Chapter Eleven

"**M**r. Sims?"

April had darted into the livery to elude Will. Then she'd walked halfway home, trying to make sense of the last three weeks. She'd finally given up—there was no understanding any of it. She just needed to accept as she'd promised herself she'd do.

She'd started thinking about her options, then headed straight back to town and the saloon, figuring that was where she'd find Lyonel Sims.

It had taken her a few attempts to gather enough courage to enter the place. She'd waited until the sun was going down, until the street had become a bit more deserted. But now she stood inside the noisy saloon, in front of the poker table where her father's partner sat with a group of men drinking whiskey and playing cards.

"Could we go outside so we can talk?" She tried to ignore the stares she received, the stench of tobacco and sweat and the raucous, raunchy banter of the men all around her. Instead she regarded the grizzled old man, who had dropped his bottom lip and regarded her with shock. "I wouldn't bother you, sir, but it is important."

Without a word Sims nodded, scooted his chair back and preceded her out the door.

April was finally able to breathe. "Let's cross the street, shall we, so we can hear each other."

Sims swayed slightly and the stench of whiskey emanated from him, but April didn't think he was too drunk.

"Wh-what ya be wantin', Miss Wilde?" he slurred. "I done told the judge ever'thin' I knows about Justus and Caulder. I wished yer Pa had done things a mite diff'rent than he did, but I couldn't change that. And he had your best interests at heart, ma'am. Truly he did."

April wasn't so sure about that but she hadn't come to argue with the man. "I understand completely, Mr. Sims. But I didn't come here to discuss my father, or your testimony. I came here because, you see, now that my sisters and I have lost our farm, we have to find a place to go. And you were my father's partner, were you not?"

"Sure was, missy."

"And you mined together, isn't that right, too?"

"Yep."

"Well, then, sir, I assume there is still a mine, and I was thinking—actually, I've made a decision and I thought you should know."

"A decision?"

"Yes. My sisters and I will be going back with you

to Cripple Creek, Mr. Sims. To work my father's portion of your—our—strike."

The man's bulbous eyes widened. He wobbled backward and fell against a hitching post. "You're gonna do what?" he shouted.

"We have no other choice, Mr. Sims," April returned calmly. "Now, I could use your assistance. We need to know what to bring. Supplies, clothes, things like that. And I'm sure, sir, we will be of benefit to you as well. Once you get used to the idea of us being around."

Will had watched April enter the saloon while sitting at the bar working on his third sarsaparilla. Disbelief had been an understatement. He'd searched for her high and low after she'd given him the slip. He'd finally given up and given in to the men pestering him to join them for a drink.

His father and cousin had already returned to the hotel after having a drink themselves. And then who had walked into the ladies' forbidden territory?

His first thought was to turn her on her heel and lead her out the door. His second was to stay where he was and watch. Him and everyone else as she walked up to Lyonel Sims and led the man away by his floor-length chin.

She hadn't given any notice to anyone else in the room—to Will. And she still didn't realize he was standing only feet away from her and Sims as she declared her intentions to leave with him for Cripple Creek.

But Will felt his insides begin to churn, and a strange sort of desperation rest inside his heart. The mining town was no place for April or her sisters.

They'd be swallowed up whole by the crowds and the filth and the depravity.

But it was obvious April hadn't listened to him say he had no intention of keeping her farm, or making her and the girls move out. She was more stubborn than she was bold and brash.

Will backed into the shadows and listened as Sims tried and tried again to dissuade her from her decision. But there was no changing April's mind. The old-timer gave up as well.

"Then it's settled. We'll begin preparing to leave tomorrow. You can return to the saloon now, Mr. Sims, if you must. Perhaps you should think about retiring, though. I'll return in the morning for you."

Sims nodded obediently. Will waited for the old miner to meander like a beaten dog toward the hotel before he himself emerged from the shadows. April was watching the prospector until she saw Will. She frowned.

"Don't you think you're being a bit foolhardy?" he asked.

She clutched her jacket around her waist and began to walk down the darkened and abandoned boardwalk. "I don't know what you're talking about, Mr. Caulder."

"You do so." He stepped into pace alongside her. "I heard everything you and Sims were discussing."

"Then you're an eavesdropper as well as a thief." She lengthened her stride. "It's obvious my father wasn't a very good judge of character."

Will rubbed his nearly-healed cut. "I won't argue with you on that point, but you know very well I'm not taking the farm."

"I don't know any such thing."

He abruptly stopped. She kept on moving. "Are you going to walk all the way home?"

"Yes."

"It's dark. It's cold."

"I have no other mode of transportation."

"You should have thought about that before you told May and June to go home without you."

His words halted her. She spun to face him, hands on hips. "I don't need any advice from you, Mr. Caulder. I *did* think about those things and I assumed I'd be home before now. But while on my way, and asking myself what I was going to do now that you got away with your thievery, I had the idea to move to Cripple Creek. I therefore obviously needed to talk with Mr. Sims."

"To coerce him into taking you?"

"I didn't coerce him," she flung back.

"You did, too. That old man didn't have a chance against you."

"You act as if I badgered him. I merely explained that Cripple Creek was our best choice, given the circumstances."

"I thought staying on the farm was your best choice."

She glared at him and growled, then began to walk away again.

Will let her go, deciding instead to double back to the saloon where Tate was tethered. He caught up to her by the time she was on the dirt road.

"Get on," he said as he rode Tate up alongside her.

April nearly slid out of her skin. She'd heard the horse approaching, had hoped the rider would just keep going, ignore her. It was foolish of her to be out on the road so late, unprotected. But she'd thought

Will had gone, had finally given up arguing with her. And then his voice had sounded in her ear.

It took her heart a moment to settle. She glanced at Tate and felt sudden relief. Then she set her chin. She wasn't about to accept Will's offer of a ride.

"No, thank you."

She heard his exasperated sigh. "Has anyone ever told you you've got a strong will of your own that's dangerous?"

"I—" Her words died in her throat. "What did you say?"

"I said you have a stubborn, strong will. One that's dangerous."

April came to an abrupt stop.

Oh, child, what a strong will you have. April, don't allow it to lead you astray.

She peered up at him, her mother's words resonating in her ears. Words she hadn't given thought to for a long time. "I—" she began again, more tentatively.

Will slid his leg over Tate's back and jumped down in front of her. "Are you all right?"

Was she being stubborn? Was she letting her pride stand in her way? Was she letting her own self-will overshadow the Will before her? He had said he loved her. Had told the entire courtroom. Had told her, in fact, that he wasn't going to take her property away from her.

She hadn't believed him. But why? Had he lied to her? Ever? She thought back to the first night when she had found him in the barn. He'd told her then and there his intent. And when he'd started expanding the house, and when he'd caught the mustang. Will had never misrepresented himself.

But he had said *he loved her.* How was she supposed to believe *that*?

"April?"

She shook herself from her contemplation but could only stare at him.

"Let me help you up on Tate so we can ride home."

"All right," she gave in. She did so because she really didn't want to walk all the way home. And her new thoughts were making it difficult to concentrate. On Tate's back, she'd have time to consider her will. And Will.

In the dimness, she could tell her answer surprised him. But he extended his hand and she took it. The warmth of his calloused palms soothed her.

"Whoa, Tate." His tone was soft, raspy. The horse held steady while Will swung her up onto his back. He then swung up behind her, wrapping his arms around her to take up the reins.

The most remarkable quiver slid through April's body. She felt it begin in her stomach, radiate down to the tips of her toes and up to the tips of her ears. When she heard what she thought was a groan from Will, the tingling recurred.

"Maybe I didn't think this idea through," he whispered into her ear. His chin was touching her hair, his chest pressed against her back. His legs brushed her own.

"I'll get down," she answered with a catch in her throat.

"No, you won't," he replied firmly, dropping his hands over hers resting on the pummel. He clicked Tate's reins and the horse began a slow walk down the darkened road. Several minutes passed with only the sound of Tate's hoofs breaking the night's silence. Most of the robins, blackbirds and blue jays had migrated south for the winter. The magpies, with their long black and blue tails and the prevalent woodpeckers, with their brilliant red wings, were settled in their nests for the night.

April wished her thoughts would settle. But they were all struggling for dominance in her brain.

"Are you going to talk to me now?" Will finally asked. His voice against her ear was sultry, warming her inside.

Instead of rashly telling him no, April considered his question. She admitted she wanted to talk to him. If only to quiet her mind. "Yes," she answered tentatively.

He exhaled quietly, blowing her hair onto her cheek. The strands tickled her ear. "Your father sure had me fooled. I still can't believe he was sick and not drunk. I keep thinking about that night, and the things that were said. Sims and Rodriguez lost a lot of money to me, you know. Which makes me think that part was all set up as well."

April struggled with Mr. Sims' story. If he was telling the truth, she had to revise every thought she'd ever had about Justus Wilde. She would have to give her father the benefit of the doubt, consider he wasn't just a deserter, but a loving father as well. Perhaps to the best of his ability. He had, after all, thought about his daughters in the end.

"He made it sound like you and May and June were still young girls. I don't think he realized how much time had passed. He hadn't a clue you were all grown women."

"But he must have. He sent you to take care of us. Isn't that what Mr. Sims said?"

He didn't respond right away. "Maybe he thought if I knew you were older I wouldn't come. He was right. I was led to believe you were still a kid. Had I known you and May and June were grown women, living alone . . ."

"You'd have never ended up in our barn?"

"Probably not."

April shuddered.

"You're cold." He squeezed his arms more tightly around her.

"I . . . no, I was just wondering what things would be like if you'd never arrived."

He smirked. "Your life wouldn't have been made a living hell."

"Yes, but . . ."

"But what? April?"

How could she tell him she might never have been put through so much anguish, but she'd have never experienced any of the thrilling emotions Will made her feel? Or that without his presence she would have never realized that *all* men weren't miserable blackguards? She would have gone on with her boring life, never experiencing anything but pain.

"But you wouldn't have been there to save me from the coyote," she finally answered in a hush.

"The coyote. Yes. At the time I thought perhaps that was the one and only reason I had been sent here. Now I know differently."

"What do you mean?" She was almost too afraid to ask, too afraid of his answer.

"I mean, Miss Wilde, saving you from the coyote was just the beginning. I learned that after Talbot and Claymore's visit."

"You were sent to save me from Cirrus, too?"

"I sure was. But more than that, I was sent to love you."

April gasped on her own intake of breath. He'd said those words again.

"You still don't believe me."

I . . . I'm trying to decide if I can believe you." April squeezed her eyes shut. "I can't think of an incident where you lied to me."

"No, and you won't."

"And I can't think of anything you've done—other than try to take the land—"

"Legally."

"That was dishonest."

"And you won't." He brought Tate to an easy halt. "April, I know you still think I'm a thief, but try to understand I've been searching for a new life since the war. I felt like such a failure for letting our plantation be destroyed. When the wager was dropped in my lap I wasn't going to let anything stop me from grabbing hold."

He placed his hand on her hip and nudged her around to face him. "When I saw what I had done to you, how maligned you had become by Cirrus and Moss and everyone else in Ruley, I changed my mind. No piece of land was worth what you were going through."

"So you went to see Judge Claymore?"

"To withdraw. He told me I'd have to do so in court. And he agreed to accept it. Actually I think he was going to rule in your favor all along. He, ah, made it clear to me—and to Mrs. Claymore—that he didn't feel the same way about you as she does."

"Really?"

"Cross my heart," he said and did it. The breeze fluttered their hair. April stared at Will as he stared back at her and the night grew quiet again. "I've been crossing my heart for awhile now," he finally went on. "Holding it together. Stitching it up, you might say."

"Why?" she whispered.

"Because one beautiful green-eyed wildflower has all but stolen it right out of my chest. And because she won't admit with words that I've stolen hers, too."

Since June had brown eyes and May had blue, April had no doubt who Will was talking about. She grinned and lowered her gaze. "You think she's admitted to you in other ways?"

"Oh, yeah," he drawled. "She's admitted it with her lips. I've never been kissed the way she kisses me. Like she can't get enough. Like she doesn't want to let go."

April blushed to her feet.

"Not that I'm complaining. Far from it. I can't get enough of her either. That's why I always find myself close to where she is."

April heard her own sob. She felt Will's finger beneath her chin, lifting it.

"Right now," he said as their gazes locked, "I couldn't bear to be anywhere but right here."

"Oh, Will," she breathed as he bent forward to taste her lips before caressing her hair, her neck.

"April, please honor me by being my wife."

His words sent another tremble through her. She clung to him, happy and terrified all at once.

"I . . . I . . . But Will, you might not want me if you knew the things . . . I prayed and prayed something would happen to make you leave. And I'm prideful. Ask Pastor Johnson. And unforgiving. And, as you pointed out, I have a strong will. My mother said the same thing. But there's only so much a person can take. It's been seven years since she died. And I've struggled through every one."

She drew in her bottom lip, then felt Will's thumb brush her lips, smoothing them back in place. Like he was telling her she didn't have to worry anymore.

"April, nothing you can say would make me change my mind. And I'd wager the farm God doesn't blame you for your prayers. I just think, maybe you were praying for the wrong thing."

"Praying for the wrong thing?"

"You said you prayed for me to leave. Not for the best thing to happen."

"I . . . You're right. I didn't. My prayer was that you'd leave. Because if I lost the farm I'd be devastated."

"Well, then, there you have it. Judge Claymore gave me the farm but I'm returning it."

"But . . . but what if my heart is still angry?"

"Is it?"

"I . . ." Was it? April had been angry for so long. But when she looked at Will now, she wasn't. When she thought about spending her life with him, the last thing she felt was anger. Had she prayed the wrong prayer? Asked for the wrong kind of help?

Had her Red Sea been parted after all?

April closed her eyes.

"Once we're married I thought you and I could move a little downstream. Build our own place." Will clicked Tate's reins, talking as if April hadn't just experienced a major revelation. And had already agreed to marry him.

"Would you mind if my family moves somewhere close? I told them awhile ago that I was going to marry you. Build another house. They're pretty pleased, you know."

She turned to look at him.

"I think you liked my family, didn't you? May and June can live in the old cabin if they aren't married by then. Your sisters will always have a place with us too. Never think they won't."

"All right." It was the only thing she could say.

"And it looks like my cousin wants to stay here, too. He wants to partner with us in our horse-training business. Since he has the capital, it would help. I spotted a pretty little mare the other night when I was out with the rust. You're going to love her. You and me—we'll bring her home soon. We'll start taming her. Together."

April felt prickly.

"Well then?" Will leaned over her shoulder.

April's heart caught. "Well then, what?"

"Are you going to marry me?"

"Do you really want me?"

"Want you?" He pulled Tate to a stop again and spun April to face him. His gaze pierced her own. "Woman, I want you more than life itself." He took her in his arms then and kissed her soundly.

When he pulled away his grin was lopsided.

"I'd love to be your wife," April told him.

Chapter Twelve

The uproar woke her.

At first April thought she was dreaming and was still back in the noisy courtroom fighting for her land. But slowly her thoughts advanced. She was with Will, on Tate's back, and . . . She smiled, remembering, and stretched in her bed. Then the commotion that had made her stir caught her ears again. She opened her eyes to find her room bright with sunlight.

How late had she slept?

Flinging the quilts aside, she padded across the cold floor and peered out her door. Voices were clearer but there was no one in the house. They were coming from the porch.

April pulled on her coat. Smoothing her hair with her hand, she crossed to the front door.

"Now hold on," she heard. Will's voice. She cracked open the door. His solid frame was standing just outside the door. "I understand your concern. It fact, I think it's long overdue. If you'll just hear me out."

April slit the door open wider and gasped when she saw the large crowd standing in the yard. "What's going on?" she asked and stepped outside.

He pivoted to face her. "Morning, sleepyhead," he smiled. "You've got company."

"Miss April, we come to demand Mr. Caulder give you back your land."

"It's not right what the judge did. It's not right what we did to you all these years. We're here to set things straight."

April peered down at the crowd. There had to be twenty people or more. Stan Elliott had been the first to speak. Yolanda Pierce the second. And April saw Mr. Dortch, Pastor Johnson, Mr. and Mrs. Layburn, and Bea and Ellie. Her legs nearly gave out.

"I've been trying to tell your new friends." Will punctuated the last word. "That things have changed a little since court yesterday." He smiled again. "You want to enlighten them?"

April gripped the edges of her coat. She couldn't believe she was standing on the porch in front of half of Ruley, with her—was it true?—husband-to-be, grinning at her like a lovesick cow. May and June were behind Will, waiting for her to say something.

"Tell them my son would never do the despicable things they claim."

April's eyes widened at the sound of Mrs. Caulder's voice. She stood with her husband in the middle of the crowd.

"He told us the day we arrived that his conscience had bothered him so much he couldn't take the property."

"No," April hurried, sympathizing with the woman. "I mean, of course he wouldn't. That is . . ." She began to chew her bottom lip, then quickly halted. Remembering that she wasn't alone anymore. She looked to Will for assistance. And then she smiled. Chuckled. She covered her mouth. "I think, Mr. Caulder, I'll leave this for you to deal with. I can now, you know?"

Will cleared his throat. "You don't say? Well, I'm glad you see things my way for a change." He slid a step closer to her and put his arm around her waist. The crowd inhaled collectively, May and June with them.

"Miss Wilde and her sisters won't be going anywhere," Will told them. "This is their land and it always will be. But I won't be going anywhere either. Except upriver a bit, when my bride and I build our own place." He turned April in his arms. He kissed her brow, then backed away as his gaze locked on hers. "I hope you all approve, of course. We'd like your blessings."

The group roared. May and June ran to April and hugged her tightly while everyone in the yard called out their best wishes.

April hugged her sisters back, tears brimming her eyes. And then she looked toward the hill—the hill where her mother lay.

The sun was high in the sky, shining brightly on the patch of dirt. April's chest tightened and her throat constricted as the past and the present mingled together to tug at her heart.

Oh, mama, she silently cried. *You knew me so well, didn't you?* Knew it would take a mighty lesson to break down her strong will. Knew there would have to be a miracle to help her understand.

She chuckled again, enjoying the new feeling, turning her attention back to her miracle. Will brushed her tears away and cupped her face.

He'd have never traveled west if not for losing everything in the war. He'd have never ended up in her barn if her father hadn't been in Cripple Creek. God *did* work in mysterious ways.

"I love you," she whispered as she sniffed.

"I love you, April." His voice was thick. "You're my beautiful wildflower."

And for the first time in a long time, even though winter was upon them, April felt certain spring had come.

Jレ